PLAYBOY'S stories of the SINISTER & STRANGE
SELECTED BY THE EDITORS OF PLAYBOY

PLAYBOY PRESS

Cover Illustration: Gilbert Stone

Published simultaneously in the United States and Canada by Playboy Press, Chicago, Illinois. Printed in the United States of America. Library of Congress Catalog Card Number: 77-78510. First edition.

contents

preface

Spine-tinglers, tales of inexplicable torment, have kept audiences from Homer, and before, spellbound as they unleashed for teller and listener alike deep-seated, primitive fears and fantasies. The simple narrative of ghosts and other mysteries has gradually grown more complex, more provocatively innovative and varied and, in this century, has resulted in the full flowering of the science-fiction story and the tale of psychological terror.

Gathered together in this volume are 11 modern spine-tinglers—contemporary, masterly stories of incredible events, inhabited by bizarre characters, told by some of the world's most gifted writers. Stories of fantasy, horror, science fiction and suspense, as well as many that cannot easily be cataloged or labeled, they are all undeniably sinister and most disquietingly strange.

Take, for example, John D. MacDonald's *The Annex*. It is not a ghost story, it cannot be called fantasy or horror in the usual genre senses, neither is it science fiction or a tale of the supernatural; but it *is* sinister and strange—and superb.

Similarly unclassifiable are Gerald Green's *The Dispatcher*, Ken W. Purdy's *The Golden Frog*, Gerald Kersh's *Somewhere Not Far from Here*.

On the other hand, some stories are pure fantasies: Bruce Jay Friedman's *The Investor*, Charles Beaumont's *The Dark Music*, G. L. Tassone's *Room 312*.

Others are definitely science fiction, representing various schools of that broad field: Kurt Vonnegut's *Welcome to the Monkey House*, John Wyndham's *Wise Child*, Ray Russell's *Ripples*, and the dramatic novella, *The Mannichon Solution*, in which Irwin Shaw reveals a bright new facet of his famous talent.

Ranging over the whole wide spectrum of *outre* fiction, differing sharply in method and mood, these stories yet are united by common bonds—all were written for PLAYBOY magazine, and all reflect Man's ambivalent love-hate affair with that fascinating, seductive siren, The Unknown.

—the editors of PLAYBOY

The Mannichon Solution/irwin shaw

One light shone late in the dark bulk of the Vogel-Paulson Research Laboratories. Mice of all colors and genetic backgrounds slept in their cages. Monkeys dozed, dogs dreamed, classified albino rats waited predictably for the morning's scalpels and injections. Computers hummed quietly, preparing gigantic responses on shadowed floors for the morrow. Cultures spread like geometric flowers in shrouded test tubes; city-states of bacteria vanished in aseptic dishes washed by scientific night; surprising serums precipitated obscurely to dash or reward the hopes of daylight. Chemicals secretly traded molecules behind pulled blinds, atoms whirled unobserved, cures and poisons formed in locked rooms. Electromagnetic tumblers guarded a million formulas in safes that reflected a gleam of steel in stray rays of moonlight.

In the one brightly lit, scrubbed room, a figure in white moved from table to table, pouring a liquid into a shallow glass receptacle, adding a puce-colored powder to the contents of a beaker, making notes on a baby-blue work pad. This was Collier Mannichon. He was medium-sized, plump, his face was melon-round, melon-smooth (he had to shave only twice a week), his high forehead, melon-bulged. Looking at him, it was impossible not to be reminded of a smooth-skinned cantaloupe, quite ripe, but not particularly tasty, and equipped with thick glasses. He had teapot-blue eyes, with the expectant expression of an infant whose diapers have been wet for some time. There was a blondish fuzz on top of the melony forehead and a small watermelon of a paunch. Collier Mannichon did not look like a Nobel Prize winner. He was not a Nobel Prize winner. He was 29 years and 3 months old. He knew that statistics showed that the majority of great scientific discoveries had been made by men before they reached their 32nd birthday. He had two years and nine months to go.

His chances of making a great scientific discovery in the Vogel-Paulson Laboratories were remote. He was in the Detergents and Solvents department. He was assigned to the task of searching for a detergent that would eventually break down in water, as there had been several unpleasant articles in national magazines recently about frothing sewers and running brooks covered with layers of suds in which trout died. Mannichon knew that nobody had ever won the Nobel Prize for inventing a new detergent, even one that did not kill trout. In one week, he would be 29 years and 4 months old.

Other men in the laboratory, younger men, were working on leukemia and cancer of the cervix and compounds that showed promise in the treatment of schizophrenia. There was even a 20-year-old prodigy who was assigned to do something absolutely secret with free hydrogen. All possible roads to Stockholm.

They were called in to high-level staff meetings, and Mr. Paulson invited them to the country club and to his home and they drove around in sports cars with pretty, lascivious girls, almost like movie actors. Mr. Paulson never came into the detergent department, and when he passed Mannichon in the corridors, he called him Jones. Somehow, six years ago, Mr. Paulson had got the idea that Mannichon's name was Jones.

Mannichon was married to a woman who looked like a casaba melon and he had two children, a boy and a girl, who looked like what you might expect them to look like, and he drove a 1959 Plymouth. His wife made no objections to his working at night. Quite the opposite.

Still, it was better than teaching chemistry in a high school.

He was working at night because he had been confronted by a puzzling reaction that afternoon. He had taken the company's standard detergent, Floxo, and added, more or less at random, some of the puce-colored powder, a comparatively simple mixture known familiarly as dioxotetramercphenoferrogene 14, which was known to combine freely with certain stearates. It was an expensive chemical and he had had some unpleasant moments with the auditing department about his budget, so he had used only one gram to a pound of Floxo, which cost $1.80 a ton to produce and was sold at all your better supermarkets for 47 cents the convenient household economy-size giant package, with Green Stamps.

He had put in a piece of white cotton waste, stained with catsup from his luncheon lettuce-and-tomato sandwich, and had been disappointed to see that while his control solution of pure Floxo had completely removed the stain from a similarly prepared piece of

cotton waste, the solution with dioxotetramercphenoferrogene 14 had left a clearly defined ring on the
cloth, which looked just like what it was, catsup.

He had tried a solution with one milligram of
dioxotetramercphenoferrogene 14, but the result had
been exactly the same. He had been working on the
project for 16 months and he was understandably a
little discouraged and was about to throw both samples
out when he saw that while the pure Floxo was suds-
ing away in its usual national-magazine-disapproved
manner, the treated mixture now looked like the most
limpid mountain spring water.

When he realized the enormity of his discovery, he
had to sit down, his knees too weak to carry him. Before his eyes danced a vision of sewers that looked just
like sewers in 1890 and trout leaping at the very
mouths of conduits leading from thickly settled hous-
ing developments. Mr. Paulson would no longer call
him Jones. He would buy a Triumph. He would get
a divorce and get fitted for contact lenses. He would be
promoted to Cancer.

All that remained to be done was to find the right
proportion of dioxotetramercphenoferrogene 14 to
Floxo, the exact ratio that would not produce post-
operational suds and at the same time not leave rings,
and his future would be assured.

Trained researcher as he was, he set about methodically, though with quick-beating heart, making one
mixture after another. He was lavish with the dioxotetramercphenoferrogene 14. This was no moment for
penny pinching. He ran out of catsup and used tobacco tar from his pipe instead. But all through the
afternoon, all through the lonely vigils of the night
(he had called his wife and told her not to wait for
dinner), the results were always the same. The telltale

ring remained. It remained on cotton. It remained on linoleum. It remained on plastic. It remained on leatherette. It remained on the back of his hand.

He did not despair. Erlich had tried 605 combinations before the magic 606th. Science was long, time nothing.

He ran out of inanimate testing materials. He took out two white mice from a batch that had been given to him because they obstinately refused to grow tumors. Vogel-Paulson was running a campaign to induce dog owners to wash their animals' coats with Floxo, because Floxo was lagging in the household field behind its greatest competitor, Wondro, and new avenues of exploitation were being called for. The results on the mice were the same as on everything else. One mouse came out as white as the day it was born and the solution it had been washed in frothed normally. The other mouse looked as though it had been branded, but the solution Mannichon had used on it clarified within five minutes.

He killed the two mice. He was a conscientious man. He didn't use second-run mice. In killing the second mouse, he had the impression of being bitten. He prepared a new solution, this time with a millionth of a gram of dioxotetramercphenoferrogene 14, and went to the cages and reached in for two more mice. He had a mixed lot in the cages. Since he got the mice that were considered scientifically useless everywhere else in the laboratories, he had mice that suffered from gigantism, blind mice, black mice, piebald mice, mice that ate their young, freakish yellow mice, gray mice with magenta spots and mice that dashed themselves to death against the bars of their cages upon hearing the note A-flat on a tuning fork.

Gingerly avoiding their fangs, he extracted two mice

from their cages. The room in which the cages were kept was in darkness, in deference to the auditing department's views on the extravagant use of electric current in Detergents and Solvents, so Mannichon didn't see the color of the mice until he brought them into his laboratory. They were yellowish in tone, almost like an off-breed golden Labrador or an unwell Chinese laundryman. He stained the mice carefully with tobacco tar. He had been smoking furiously to produce enough tobacco tar and his tongue was raw, but this was no time to balk at sacrifice.

He put one mouse in an inch of Floxo and distilled water and washed it carefully, after running alcohol over his hands. The mouse splashed brightly, seeming to enjoy its bath, as the stain vanished and the suds fizzed. He put the other mouse into a similar mixture and added a millionth of a gram of dioxotetramerc-phenoferrogene 14. He washed his hands again in alcohol. When he turned back to the second mouse, he saw that it had fallen over on its side into the solution. He bent over and peered at the mouse. It was not breathing. It was dead. He had seen enough dead mice to know a dead mouse when he saw one. He felt a wave of irritation with the organization of the laboratory. How did they expect him to get any serious work done when they gave him mice that collapsed at the first touch of the human hand?

He disposed of the dead mouse and went into the next room for a fresh one. This time, he turned on the light. The hell with those bastards in Audit.

Moved by one of those flashes of inspiration that reason cannot explain but which have made for such leaps forward in the sciences, he picked out another yellowish mouse, a sister of the one that had died. Defiantly, he left the light on in the mouse room, which began to tweak at about eight decibels.

Back in the laboratory, he carefully anointed the new mouse with tobacco tar, noticing meanwhile that the first mouse was still happily frisking in its invigorating suds. He put the mouse he was carrying down in an empty glass dish, its sides just a little too high for jumping. Then he poured some of the mixture with dioxotetramercphenoferrogene 14 in it over the new mouse. For a moment, nothing happened. He watched closely, his face six inches from the glass pan. The mouse sighed and lay down quietly and died.

Mannichon sat up. He stood up. He lit a new pipe. He went to the window. He looked out the window. The moon was sinking behind a chimney. He puffed on his pipe. Somewhere here, he sensed with his scientist's trained intuition, there was a cause and there was an effect. The effect was fairly evident. Two dead mice. But the first mouse, the white mouse, that he had put into practically the same solution, had not died, even though the stain had remained in its fur. White mouse, yellow mouse, yellow mouse, white mouse. Mannichon's head began to ache. The moon disappeared behind the chimney.

Mannichon went back to the table. The dead yellow mouse in one pan was already stiffening, looking peaceful in the clear, clean-looking liquid. In the other pan, the other yellow mouse was surfing on the pure Floxo suds. Mannichon removed the dead mouse and put it into the refrigerator for future reference.

He went back into the mouse room, now tweaking at 11 decibels. He brought back with him a gray mouse, a black mouse and a piebald mouse. Without bothering to stain them, he put them one by one into the solution in which the two yellow mice had died. They all seemed to relish the immersion and the piebald mouse was so frisky after it that it attempted to mate with the black mouse, even though they were both males. Mannichon put all three control mice back into portable cages and then stared hard and long at the yellow mouse, still basking in its miniature Mediterranean of foamy, never-failing Floxo.

Mannichon gently lifted the yellow mouse out of the suds. He dried it thoroughly, which seemed to irritate the beast. Somehow, Mannichon got the impression that he had been bitten again. Then he carefully let the yellow mouse down into the pan in which his two yellow brethren had died and in which the three varicolored control mice had sported.

For a moment, nothing happened. Then, in his turn, the yellow mouse in the middle of the pan sighed and lay down and died.

Mannichon's headache made him close his eyes for 60 seconds. When he opened them, the yellow mouse was still dead, lying as it had fallen in the crystal-clear liquid.

Mannichon was assailed by a great weariness. Nothing like this had ever occurred to him in all the years he had been serving the cause of science. He was too tired to try to figure out what had been happening, whether it was for the better or for the worse, whether it advanced detergents or put them back 100 years, whether it moved him, Mannichon, closer to Cancer or back to Floor Wax and Glues, or even to severance pay. His brain refused to cope with the problem any longer that night and he mechanically put the dead mouse next to its mate in the refrigerator, tabbed the gray mouse, the black mouse and the piebald mouse, cleaned up, wrote his notes, put out the lights and started for home.

He didn't have the Plymouth tonight, because his

wife had needed it to go to play bridge, and all the buses had long since stopped running and he couldn't afford a taxi, even if he could have found one at that hour, so he walked home. On his way, he passed the Plymouth, parked in front of a darkened house on Sennett Street, more than a mile away from his home. Mannichon's wife had not told him whose home she was playing bridge in and he didn't recognize the house and he was surprised that people would still be playing bridge at two o'clock in the morning and with the curtains so tightly drawn that no beam of light shone through. But he didn't go in. His presence when she was playing bridge, his wife said, upset her bidding.

. . .

"Collect your notes," Samuel Crockett was saying, "and put them in your briefcase and lock it. And lock the refrigerator." There were now 18 dead yellow mice in the refrigerator. "I think we'd better talk about this someplace where we won't be disturbed."

It was the next afternoon. Mannichon had called in Crockett, who worked in the laboratory next door, at 11 A.M. Mannichon had arrived at the lab at 6:30 A.M., unable to sleep, and had spent the morning dipping everything yellow he could find into the solution, which Crockett had begun calling the Mannichon solution at 2:17 P.M. It was the first time anything had been called after Mannichon (his two children were named after his father-in-law and his mother-in-law) and Mannichon was beginning, dimly, to see himself as a Figure in the World of Science. He had already decided to get himself fitted for contact lenses before they came to photograph him for the national magazines.

Crockett, or "Crock," as he was called, was one of

the young men who drove around in an open sports car with lascivious girls. It was only a Lancia, but it was open. He had been top man in his class at MIT and was only 25 years and 3 months old and he was working on voluntary crystals and complex protein molecules, which was, in the Vogel-Paulson hierarchy, like being a marshal on Napoleon's staff. He was a lean, wiry Yankee who knew which side his experimental bread was buttered on. After the long morning of dipping bits of yellow everything (yellow silk, yellow cotton, yellow blotting paper) into the solution, with no reaction whatsoever, and executing more than a dozen yellow mice, Mannichon had felt the need for another mind and had gone next door, where Crockett had been sitting with his feet up on a stainless-steel laboratory table, chewing on a cube of sugar soaked in LSD and listening to Thelonious Monk on a portable phonograph.

There had been an initial burst of irritation. "What the hell do you want, Flox?" Crockett had said. Some of the younger men called Mannichon "Flox" as a form of professional banter. But then Crockett had consented to come along, after Mannichon had sketched out the nature of his visit. Enlisting Crockett's help had already paid off handsomely. He had had the dazzling idea at 1:57 P.M. of introducing drops of the solution orally to various colored mice, ending up with a yellow mouse, nearly the last of the batch in Mannichon's cages. The white mice, the gray mice, the black mice, the piebald mice had reacted with vigor after a few drops of the solution, becoming gay and belligerent. The yellow mouse had quietly died 28 minutes after its drink. So now they knew the solution worked internally as well as externally. However, Crockett had not yet come up with any ideas on how to erase the telltale ring that remained after the solution was used to take out stains. He didn't seem to be too interested in that aspect of the problem. But he had been impressed by the way even the smallest proportion of dioxotetramercphenoferrogene 14 had reduced the stubborn Floxo suds and had complimented Mannichon in his terse Yankee way. "You've got something there," he had said, sucking on an LSD sugar cube.

"Why can't we talk here?" Mannichon said as Crockett made preliminary moves to get out of the laboratory. Mannichon punched in and punched out and he didn't want the personnel department coming asking him why he had taken half a Thursday afternoon off.

"Don't be naïve, Flox," was all Crockett said by way of explanation. So Mannichon put all his notes in his briefcase, arranged on shelves all the apparatus and supplies they had been using, locked the refrigerator and followed Crockett out into the corridor.

They met Mr. Paulson near the front gate. "Crock, old Crock," Mr. Paulson said, putting his arm fondly around Crockett's shoulder. "My boy. Hello, Jones. Where the hell are you going?"

"I——" Mannichon began, knowing he was going to stutter.

"Appointment at an optician's," Crockett said crisply. "I'm driving him."

"Aha," said Mr. Paulson. "Science has a million eyes. Good old Crock."

They went out the front gate.

"Aren't you taking your car, Mr. Jones?" the parking-lot attendant asked Mannichon. Four years before, he had heard Mr. Paulson call Mannichon "Jones."

"Here," Crockett cut in. He gave the parking-lot

attendant a cube of LSD sugar as a tip. "Suck it."

"Thanks, Mr. Crockett." The parking-lot attendant popped the cube into his mouth and began to suck it. The Lancia swooped out of the lot onto the highway, Italian, the Via Veneto, national magazines, the Affluent Society, open to the sun, wind and rain. Ah, God, Mannichon thought, this is the way to live.

• • •

"Now," said Crockett, "let's add up the pluses and the minuses."

They were sitting in a dark bar, decorated like an English coaching inn, curled brass horns, whips, hunting prints. At carefully spaced intervals along the mahogany bar, three married ladies sat in miniskirts, waiting for gentlemen who were not their husbands. Crockett was drinking Jack Daniel's and water. Mannichon sipped at an alexander, the only alcoholic drink he could get down, because it reminded him of a milk shake.

"Plus one," Crockett said. "No suds. Enormous advantage. The polluted rivers of the world. You will be hailed as a Cultural Hero."

Mannichon began to sweat pleasurably.

"Minus one," Crockett went on, waving for another Jack Daniel's. He drank fast. "Minus one—residual rings. Not an insuperable obstacle, perhaps."

"Question of time," Mannichon murmured. "With different catalysts, we might——"

"Perhaps," Crockett said. "Plus two. Distinct affinity, as yet unclear, to yellow living organisms, so far essentially confined to mice. Further experiment clearly indicated along this line. Still, a breakthrough. All specific chemical affinities with diverse particularized organisms eagerly sought after. Definitely a breakthrough. You will be praised."

"Well, Mr. Crockett," Mannichon said, sweating with even more pleasure, hearing language like that from a man who had been first in his year at MIT, "it certainly is——"

"Call me Crock," Crockett said. "We're in this together."

"Crock," Mannichon said gratefully, thinking of the Lancia.

"Minus two," Crockett said, accepting the fresh Jack Daniel's from the waiter. "Solution seems to be fatal to organisms for which it shows affinity. Question is—is it really a minus?"

"It's . . . well . . . unsettling," Mannichon said, thinking of the 18 rigid mice in the locked refrigerator.

"Negative reactions sometimes positive reactions in disguise. Depends upon point of view," Crockett said. "Natural cycle one of repair *and* destruction. Each at its own time in its own place. Mustn't lose sight."

"No," said Mannichon humbly, determined not to lose sight.

"Commercially," Crockett said. "Look at DDT. Myxomatosis. Invaluable in Australia. Overrun by rabbits. I didn't like that goldfish, though."

They had borrowed a goldfish off the desk of a receptionist and at 12:56 P.M. had put it first in pure Floxo and then in the Mannichon solution. It couldn't be said that the goldfish had seemed to *enjoy* the Floxo —it had stood on its head at the bottom on the pan and shuddered every 36 seconds—but it had lived. After 20 seconds in the Mannichon solution, it had expired. It was in the refrigerator now, with the 18 mice.

"No," Crockett repeated, "I didn't like the goldfish. Not at all."

They sat in silence, regretting the goldfish.

"Recapitulation," Crockett said. "We are in possession of formula with unusual qualities. Breaks down tensile balance of otherwise cohesive liquid molecules at normal temperatures. Laughably cheap to manufacture. Mineral traces in minute quantities almost impossible to identify. Highly toxic to certain, specific organisms, benevolent to others. I don't know how—yet—but somewhere here, there's a dollar to be made. I have a hunch . . . a hunch. There may be a place we can. . . ." He stopped, almost as if he couldn't trust Mannichon with his thoughts. "Yellow, yellow, yellow. What the hell is yellow that we are overrun with, like rabbits in Australia? We answer that question, we can clean up."

"Well," said Mannichon, "I suppose we would be in for a raise at the end of the year from Mr. Paulson. At least a bonus at Christmas."

"A bonus?" Crockett's voice rose for the first time. "A raise? Are you mad, man?"

"Well, my contract says that everything I develop is the property of Vogel-Paulson. In exchange for—— Doesn't your contract read the same?"

"What are you, man?" Crockett asked disgustedly. "A Presbyterian?"

"Baptist," Mannichon said.

"Now you see why we had to get out of the laboratory to talk?" Crockett demanded.

"Well," said Mannichon, looking around at the bar and at the three wives in miniskirts, "I suppose this atmosphere is cozier than——"

"Cozier!" Crockett said. Then he used a rude word. "Don't you have a company, man?"

"A company?" Mannichon said, puzzled. "What would I do with a company? I make seventy-eight hundred dollars a year and what with withholding taxes and child psychiatrists and insurance. . . . Do you have a company?"

"Four, five. Maybe seven," Crockett said. "Who keeps track? One in Liechtenstein, two in the Bahamas, one in the name of a divorced nymphomaniac aunt in Ischia. Do I have a company!"

"At your age," Mannichon said admiringly. "But what are they *for*?"

"Oh, I throw Paulson a bone from time to time," Crockett said. "A low-temperature treatment for polyesters, a crystallization process for storing unstable amino acids, bagatelles like that. Paulson slobbers in gratitude. But for anything big, man, you don't think I go trotting up to the front office, wagging my tail like a bird dog with a quail in its jaws. Christ, man, where've you been? Man, I have four patents in a company's name for the hardening of glass fibers in Germany alone. And as for low-grade bauxite. . . ."

"You don't have to go into detail," Mannichon said, not wishing to seem inquisitive. He was beginning to understand where the Lancias and Corvettes and Mercedes in the laboratory parking lot came from.

"We'll set up a company in Guernsey," Crockett said. "You and I, and whoever else we need. I'm well placed in Guernsey and the bastards speak English. And for any subcompanies that come along, we can use my aunt in Ischia."

"Do you think we'll need anybody else?" Mannichon asked anxiously. In the space of ten minutes, he had acquired the first healthy instinct of a capitalist, not to share wealth unnecessarily.

"I'm afraid so," said Crockett, brooding. "We'll need a first-rate pathologist to tell us just how the Mannichon solution links up with the nuclear material of

whatever cells it has an affinity for and how it pene-
trates the cell wall. We'll need a crackerjack biochem-
ist. And an expert fieldworker to examine how the
product behaves in a free environment. This is big,
man. No use wasting time on bums. And then, of
course, the angel."

"The angel?" Mannichon was at sea. Up to then,
religion hadn't seemed to be an integral part of the
operation.

"The moneybags," Crockett said impatiently. "All
this is going to cost a packet. We can use the laboratory
for a lot of things, but finally, we have to set up on our
own."

"Of course," Mannichon said, his vocabulary as well
as his vision enlarged.

"First, the pathologist," Crockett said. "The best
man in the country is right in the shop. Good old
Tageka Kyh."

Mannichon nodded. Tageka Kyh had been top man
in his year at Kyoto and then top man at Berkeley.
He drove a Jaguar XK-E. Tageka Kyh had spoken to
him. Once. In a movie. Tageka Kyh had said, "Is this
seat taken?" Mannichon had said, "No." He remembered the exchange.

"OK," Crockett said. "Let's go catch Kyh before he
goes home. No sense in wasting time." He left a ten-
dollar bill on the table and Mannichon followed him
toward the door, feeling the attractiveness of wealth.
He passed the three wives at the bar. One day soon,
he thought, a woman like that will be waiting for me
at a bar. He shivered deliciously.

On the way to the laboratory, they bought a goldfish
for the receptionist. They had promised to bring her
fish back. She was attached to it, she said.

• • •

"Interesting, interesting," Tageka Kyh was saying. He had riffled quickly through Mannichon's notes and taken a flat, Oriental glance at the 18 mice in the refrigerator. They were in Mannichon's lab. Crockett was sure that his room and Tageka Kyh's were bugged and that Paulson ran the tapes every night. They all agreed that nobody would bother bugging Detergents and Solvents, so they could speak freely, although in lowered voices.

"Interesting," Tageka Kyh repeated. He spoke perfect English, with a Texas accent. He had put on "no" plays in San Francisco and was an authority on tobacco mosaic. "The cut is as follows. If there ever *is* a cut. All partners share equally and I have exclusive rights to Guatemala and Costa Rica."

"Kyh," Crockett protested.

"I have certain connections in the Caribbean I have to consider," Tageka Kyh said. "Take it or leave it, pardner."

"OK," Crockett said. Tageka was a lot closer to the Nobel Prize than Crockett and had companies in Panama, Nigeria and Zurich.

Tageka Kyh offhandedly slipped the tray of dead mice out of the refrigerator and the single goldfish on a flat aluminum shovel.

"Excuse me," Mannichon said. A thought had just occurred to him. "I don't like to interfere, but they're yellow—the mice, I mean——" He was sweating now, and not pleasurably. "What I'm trying to say is that up to now, at least, the . . . uh . . . the solution. . . ." Later, he would be able to say the Mannichon solution without blushing, but he wasn't up to that yet. "That is," he went on, stuttering, "the solution so far has been toxic only to . . . uh . . . organisms whose dominant, as it were, pigment, in a manner of speaking, might be described as . . . well . . . yellowish."

"What are you trying to say, pardner?" Tageka Kyh said, wintry-Texas and pre-Perry samurai at one and the same time.

"It's just that, well," Mannichon stammered, sorry he had started this, "well, there might be certain dangers. Rubber gloves, at the very least. Complete asepsis, if I might presume to advise. I'm the last man in the world to dwell on racial . . . uh . . . characteristics, but I'd feel guilty if anything . . . well, you know, if anything *happened*, as it were. . . ."

"Don't you worry about your little yellow brother, pardner," Tageka Kyh said evenly. He went out carrying the tray and the aluminum shovel debonairly, like an old judo trophy.

"Grasping bastard," Crockett said bitterly as the door closed behind the pathologist. "Exclusive rights to Guatemala *and* Costa Rica. The Rising Sun. March into Manchuria. Just like the last time."

As he drove home, Mannichon had the impression that Crockett and Tageka Kyh, though confronted with the same data as himself, somehow were leaping to conclusions still very much hidden from him. That's why they drive Lancias and Jaguars, he thought.

• • •

The telephone rang at three in the morning. Mrs. Mannichon groaned as Mannichon reached blearily over her to pick it up. She didn't like him to touch her without warning.

"Crockett here," said the voice on the phone. "I'm at Tageka's. Get over here." He barked out the address. "Pronto."

Mannichon hung up and staggered out of bed and started to dress. He had heartburn from the alexander.

"Where going?" Mrs. Mannichon said in a non-melony voice.

"Conference."

"At three in the morning?" She didn't open her eyes, but her mouth certainly moved.

"I haven't looked at the time," Mannichon said, thinking, Not for long, oh, Lord, not for long.

"Good night, Romeo," Mrs. Mannichon said, her eyes still closed.

"That was Samuel Crockett," Mannichon said, fumbling with his pants.

"Fag," Mrs. Mannichon said. "I always knew it."

"Now, Lulu. . . ." After all, Crockett was his partner.

"Bring home some LSD," Mrs. Mannichon said, falling asleep.

Now, that was a funny thing for her to say, Mannichon thought as he softly closed the door of the split-level behind him so as not to awaken the children. Both of the children had a deeply rooted fear of sudden noises, the child psychiatrist had told him.

• • •

Tageka Kyh lived downtown in the penthouse apartment of a 13-story building. His Jaguar was parked in front, and Crockett's Lancia. Mannichon parked the Plymouth behind his partners' cars, thinking, Maybe a Ferrari.

Mannichon had to admit to himself that he was surprised when he was let into the apartment by a Negro butler in a yellow striped vest and immaculate white shirt sleeves with large gold cuff links. Mannichon had expected a severe modern decor, perhaps with a Japanese touch—bamboo mats, ebony headrests, washy prints of rainy bridges on the walls. But it was all done in pure Cape Cod—chintz, cobbler's benches, captain's chairs, scrubbed pine tables, lamps made out of ships' binnacles. Poor man, Mannichon thought, he is trying to assimilate.

Crockett was waiting in the living room, drinking beer and standing looking at a full-rigged clipper ship in a bottle on the mantel.

"Hi," Crockett said. "Have a nice trip?"

"Well," Mannichon said, rubbing at his red eyes behind his glasses, "I must confess I'm not completely on the *qui vive*. I'm used to eight hours' sleep and——"

"Got to learn to cut it down," Crockett said. "I do on two." He drank some beer. "Good old Tageka'll be ready for us any minute. He's in his lab."

A door opened and a lascivious girl in tight silk off-mauve pants came in with some more beer and a plate of chocolate marshmallow cookies. She smiled lasciviously at Mannichon as she offered him the tray. He took a beer and two cookies for her sake.

"His," Crockett said.

"You bet," said the girl.

Oh, to be a Japanese pathologist, Mannichon thought.

A buzzer rang dimly. "Captain Ahab," said the girl. "He's ready for you. You know the way, Sammy."

"This way, Flox," Crockett said, starting out of the room.

"Got some, Sammy?" the girl asked.

Crockett tossed her a sugar cube. She was lying down, with her off-mauve legs high over the back of a ten-foot-long chintz couch and nibbling on the sugar with small white teeth before they were out of the room.

Tageka Kyh's laboratory was bigger and more elaborately equipped than any at Vogel-Paulson. There was a large operating table that could be rotated to any position, powerful lamps on pulleys and swivels, banks of instrument cases, sterilizers, refrigerators with glass doors, a gigantic X-ray machine, stainless-steel sinks and tables and basins, strobomicroscopes, the lot.

"Wow!" Mannichon said, standing at the door, taking it in.

"Ford," Tageka said. He was dressed in a surgeon's apron and he was pulling off a surgeon's mask and cap. Under his apron, Mannichon could see the rolled-up ends of blue jeans and high-heeled, silver-worked cowboy boots. "Well," Tageka said, "I've been teasing away at our problem." He poured himself a tumbler of California sherry from a gallon jug in a corner and drank thirstily. "I've dissected the eighteen mice. Yellow." He smiled at Mannichon with a gleam of samurai teeth. "I've looked at the slides. It's too early to say anything definite yet, Mannichon; all I can offer is an educated guess, but you've hit on something brand-new."

"Have I?" Mannichon said eagerly. "What is it?"

Tageka Kyh and Crockett exchanged significant glances, the born big-leaguers noting with pity and understanding the entrance of the born bush leaguer into the locker room. "I'm not quite sure yet, pardner," Tageka Kyh said gently. "All I'm sure of is that whatever it is, it's new. And we live in an age in which being new is enough. Remember Man Tan, remember the hula hoop, remember No-Cal, remember the stereoscope glasses for three-dimensional films. Fortunes were made. In the space of months." Mannichon began to pant. Tageka shed his apron. Under it he was wearing a Hawaiian shirt. "My preliminary conclusions," he said briskly. "A nontoxic substance, to be designated, for the sake of convenience, as Floxo, combined with another known nontoxic substance, dioxotetramercphenoferrogene 14, shows a demonstrable swift affinity for the pigment material of eighteen yellowish mice and one goldfish——"

"Nineteen," Mannichon said, remembering the first yellow mouse he had thrown into the incinerator.

"Eighteen," Tageka said. "I don't work on hearsay."

"I'm sorry," said Mannichon.

"Examination of cells," Tageka went on, "and other organs leads to the observation that in a manner as yet undiscovered, the solution unites with the pigmental matter in the cells, whose chemical formula I shall not at this moment trouble you with, to produce a new compound, formula to be ascertained, that attacks, with great speed and violence, the sympathetic nervous system, leading to almost immediate nonfunctioning of that system and subsequent stoppage of breathing, movement and heartbeat." He poured himself another tumbler of sherry. "Why are your eyes so red, pardner?"

"Well, I'm used to eight hours of sleep a night and——" Mannichon said.

"Learn to cut down," Tageka said. "I do on one."

"Yes, sir," Mannichon said.

"What practical use can be made of this interesting relationship between our solution and certain organic pigments is not within my province," Tageka said. "I'm merely a pathologist. But I am sure a bright young man can come up with a suggestion. Nothing is useless in the halls of science. After all, the Curies discovered the properties of radium because a key left overnight in a darkened room with a lump of refined pitchblende allowed its photograph to be taken. After all, nobody is much interested in taking photographs of keys, are they, pardner?" He giggled unexpectedly.

Japanese are funny, Mannichon thought. They are not like us.

Tageka grew serious again. "Further exhaustive investigation, carefully controlled, will perhaps enlighten us. Experiments with at least five hundred other yellow mice, to begin with, with five hundred controls. A thousand goldfish, similar procedure. Naturally yellow organisms, such as daffodils, parrots, squash, corn, etc., similar procedure. Higher vertebrates, dogs, a certain yellow-bottomed baboon, to be found in the rain forests of New Guinea, unfortunately rare, two horses, roans will do——"

"How can I get two horses into Detergents and Solvents?" Mannichon asked, his head reeling. "Especially if we have to keep this quiet?"

"This laboratory"—Tageka made a courteous eastwind gesture of his hand at the gleam around them—"is at the service of my honorable friends. And we must show a certain amount of initiative in conducting some of our experiments in other localities. All I need is a few correctly prepared tissue slides, stained as I direct."

"But I can't put in request forms for baboons and horses," Mannichon said, sweating again.

"I had thought it understood that we would undertake this privately," Tageka said frostily, looking at Crockett.

"That's right," Crockett said.

"But where's the money going to come from? Yellow-bottomed baboons, for God's sake," Mannichon cried.

"I am merely a pathologist," Tageka said. He drank some more sherry.

"I'm in," Crockett said.

"You can be in," Mannichon said, near tears. "You have companies all over the world. Liechtenstein, Ischia. . . . I make seven thousand eight hundred dollars a——"

"We know what you make, pardner," Tageka said.

"I will absorb your share of the preliminary expenses along with my own."

Mannichon breathed heavily with gratitude. There was no doubt about it, he was finally in with Class.

"I hardly know what to say. . . ." he began.

"There is no need to say anything," said Tageka. "As partial reimbursement for funds laid out, I shall take the exclusive rights of your share of all of northern Europe for the first ten years, on a line drawn from London to Berlin."

"Yes, sir," said Mannichon. He would have liked to say something else, but what came out was, "Yes, sir."

"I reckon that's about it for the night, pardners," Tageka said. "I don't like to rush you, but I have some work to do before I go to sleep."

He escorted Crockett and Mannichon politely to the door of the laboratory. They heard it lock behind them.

"The Oriental mind," Crockett said. "Always so suspicious."

The girl in the off-mauve pants was still lying on the couch. Her eyes were open, but she didn't seem to see anything.

There's no doubt of it, Mannichon thought, taking a last devouring look at the girl, this is the age of specialization.

• • •

The next weeks were frantic. Mannichon spent his days in Detergents and Solvents writing up reports on nonexistent experiments to indicate on the weekly reviews that he was earning his salary and loyally advancing the interests of Vogel-Paulson. The nights were spent in Tageka Kyh's laboratory. Mannichon had got his sleep down to three hours. The tests went on methodically. The 500 yellow mice duly succumbed. A yellow Afghan with an illustrious pedigree, bought at great expense, lasted less than an hour after lapping up several drops of Mannichon's solution in a bowl of milk, while a black-and-white mongrel liberated from the pound for three dollars barked happily for two days after sharing the same meal. Dead goldfish lay by the hundreds in Tageka's refrigerators and the yellow-bottomed baboon, after showing deep affection for Tageka, tolerance for Crockett and a desire to murder Mannichon, was laid to rest only ten minutes after its relevant parts had been laved in a purposely weakened variant of the solution.

During this period, Mannichon's domestic situation was not all that it might have been. His nightly absences had begun to annoy Mrs. Mannichon. He could not tell her what he was doing, except that he was working with Crockett and Tageka. Because of the community-property laws, he was planning to divorce her before the company showed any profit.

"What have you fellows got going up there every night?" Mrs. Mannichon demanded. "A rainbow-colored daisy chain?"

One more cross to bear, Mannichon thought. Temporarily.

•   •   •

Flowers and vegetables had not been affected by the solution and they had not yet tried horses. And despite some ingenious manipulations of the solution by Crockett (he had managed to subtract two hydrocarbon molecules from Floxo and had bombarded dioxotetramercphenoferrogene 14 with a large variety of radioactive isotopes), the residual ring always remained on whatever materials they tried, even after exhaustive scrubbing. While the two other men worked on serenely, checking all leads meticulously night after night and producing dazzling results for Vogel-Paulson day after day, Mannichon, vertiginous from lack of sleep, was beginning to despair of ever finding any practical use for the Mannichon solution. He would write a little paper that might or might not get published, two or three biochemists throughout the country might thumb through the pages offhandedly and another curious little dead end of research would be closed out and forgotten. He would drive the 1959 Plymouth for the rest of his life and he would never see the inside of a divorce court.

He didn't communicate his fears to Crockett and Tageka Kyh. It was hard to communicate *anything* to them. In the beginning, they rarely listened when he talked, and after a couple of weeks, they didn't listen at all. He did his work in silence. His work finally consisted of washing up, taking dictation and filing slides. He was having his troubles at Vogel-Paulson, too. His weekly running digests of nonexistent experiments were not being received with enthusiasm and an ominous memo had come to him in a baby-blue envelope from Mr. Paulson himself. "Well?" Mr. Paulson had scrawled on a large piece of paper. Just that. It was not promising.

He had decided to quit. He had to quit. He needed at least one night's sleep. He wanted to announce it to his partners, but it was difficult to find the appropriate time. He knew he couldn't say it in front of Tageka Kyh, who was a remote man, but there was a chance that if he got Crockett alone for a minute or two, he could get it out. After all, Crockett was white.

So he took to tagging after Crockett and lying in wait for him whenever he could. But it took nearly another week before his opportunity presented itself. He was waiting in front of the restaurant where Crockett often lunched, usually with a lascivious girl

or several lascivious girls. The restaurant was called
La Belle Provençale and a meal there never cost less
than ten dollars. That is, if you didn't order wine.
Mannichon had never eaten there, of course. He took
his lunch at the Vogel-Paulson commissary. You could
eat there for 85 cents. That was one good thing about
Vogel-Paulson.

It was a hot day and there was no shade. Because of
his vertigo, Mannichon rocked from side to side as he
waited, as though he were on the deck of a heaving
ship. Then he saw the Lancia drive up. For once,
Crockett was alone. He left the motor running as he
stepped out and turned the car over to the attendant
to park. He didn't notice Mannichon as he strode
toward the door of La Belle Provençale, although he
passed within three feet of him.

"Crock," Mannichon said.

Crockett stopped and looked around. A look of dis-
pleasure angled across the Yankee angles of his face.
"What the hell are you doing here?" he said.

"Crock," Mannichon said, "I have to talk to
you——"

"What the hell're you rocking for?" Crockett asked.
"Are you drunk?"

"That's one of the things I wanted to——"

A funny expression, intense and cold, came over
Crockett's face. He was staring past Mannichon, over
Mannichon's shoulder. "Look!" he said.

"You fellers've been great and all that," Mannichon
said, lurching closer to Crockett, "but I have to——"

Crockett grabbed him by the shoulders and swung
him around. "I said *look*!"

Mannichon sighed and looked. There was nothing
much to look at. Across the street, in front of a bar,
there was a broken-down old wagon full of empty

ginger-ale bottles and an old horse, its head drooping in the heat.

"Look at what, Crock?" Mannichon said. He was now seeing double, but he didn't want to burden Crockett with his troubles.

"The horse, man, the horse."

"What about the horse, Crock?"

"What color is it, man?"

"They're yellow. I mean, *it's* yellow," Mannichon said, correcting for his double vision.

"Everything comes to him who waits," Crockett said. He took out a small bottle of the Mannichon solution. He never went anyplace without it. He was a dedicated scientist, not one of those timeservers who lock their minds when they lock their office doors. Swiftly, Crockett poured some of the solution on his right hand. He gave Mannichon the bottle to hold, in case the police ever asked any questions. Then he sauntered across the street toward the old yellow horse and the wagon full of empty ginger-ale bottles. It was the first time Mannichon had seen Crockett saunter anywhere.

Crockett went up to the horse. The driver was nowhere in sight. A Buick passed with a colored man at the wheel, but aside from that, the street was empty.

"Good old dobbin," Crockett said. He patted the horse kindly on the muzzle with his wet hand. Then he sauntered back toward Mannichon. "Put that goddamn bottle in your pocket, man," he whispered. He took Mannichon's arm, wiping the last drops of the liquid off on Mannichon's sleeve. It looked friendly, but the fingers felt like steel hooks. Mannichon put the bottle of the solution in his pocket and, side by side, he and Crockett went into the restaurant.

The bar of La Belle Provencale was parallel to the

front window and the bottles were arranged on glass shelves up against the window. With the light from the street coming in from behind them, the bottles looked like jewelry. It was an artistic effect. There were quite a few people eating ten-dollar lunches in the dark interior of the restaurant, in a hush of expensive French food, but there was nobody else at the bar. The room was air conditioned and Mannichon shivered uncontrollably as he sat on the bar stool, looking out at the street through the bottles. He could see the yellow horse between a bottle of Chartreuse and a bottle of Noilly-Prat. The yellow horse hadn't moved. He was still there in the heat with his head down.

"What'll it be, Mr. Crockett?" the bartender said. "The usual?" Everybody always knew Crockett's name.

"The usual, Benny," Crockett said. "And an alexander for my friend." Crockett never forgot anything.

They watched the horse through the bottles while Benny prepared the Jack Daniel's and the alexander. The horse didn't do anything.

The bartender served the drinks and Crockett drank half of his in one gulp. Mannichon sipped at his alexander. "Crock," he said, "I really do have to talk to you. This whole thing is getting me——"

"Sssh," Crockett said. The driver of the wagon was coming out of the bar across the street. He climbed up onto the seat of the wagon and picked up the reins. The horse slowly went down on its knees and then all the way down between the traces. The horse didn't move anymore.

"Send two more drinks to the table, Benny," Crockett said. "Come on, Flox, I'll buy you lunch."

Crockett ordered *tripes à la mode de Caen* for lunch and a bottle of hard cider. Crockett certainly wasn't a typical Yankee. As soon as Mannichon saw and smelled the dish, he knew his stomach was going to make some peculiar claims on his attention that afternoon. He never did quite manage to tell Crockett that he wanted to quit.

• • •

"Now for the next step," Tageka Kyh was saying. All three of them were in his laboratory in the penthouse. It was comparatively early, only 2:30 A.M. Tageka had taken the news about the horse without surprise, although he did say that it was too bad they hadn't gotten any slides. "We've gone just about as far as necessary with the lower vertebrates," Tageka Kyh said. "The next experiment suggests itself inevitably."

It didn't suggest itself inevitably to Mannichon. "What's that?" he said.

For once, Tageka Kyh answered one of Mannichon's questions. "Man," he said simply.

Mannichon opened his mouth and kept it open. He didn't close it for some time.

Crockett had his face squeezed up into lines of concentration. "I foresee certain complications," he said.

"Nothing serious," Tageka Kyh said. "All it needs is access to a hospital with a decent selection of pigmented subjects."

"Well, I know everybody at Lakeview General downtown, of course," Crockett said, "but I don't think we'd find the proper range. After all, we're in the Midwest. I doubt if you'd even find more than two or three Indians in a year."

Mannichon still had his mouth open.

"I don't trust those fellows at General," Tageka Kyh said. "They're sloppy. And whatever man we pick we'll have to bring in as a full partner, of course, and I don't like anyone down at General enough to dump a fortune in his lap."

Mannichon would have liked to interrupt at this point. Tageka Kyh's use of the word fortune seemed careless, to say the least. Everything they had done up to now, as far as Mannichon was concerned, had been rigorously devoid of all possibility of profit. But Tageka Kyh was caught up in his planning, speaking smoothly, articulating well, pronouncing every syllable.

"I think all indications point to the West Coast. San Francisco comes to mind," Tageka Kyh said. "A sizable nonwhite population, well-run hospitals with large nonsegregated charity wards. . . ."

"Chinatown," Mannichon said. He had been there on his honeymoon. He had had shark's-fin soup. You only get married once, he had said to Lulu.

"I have a friend on the staff of Mercy and Cancer," Tageka Kyh said. "Ludwig Qvelch."

"Of course," Crockett nodded. "Qvelch. Prostate. Top-notch." Crockett had heard of everybody.

"He was first in his class at Berkeley three years before me," Tageka Kyh said. "I think I'll give him a tinkle." He reached for the phone.

"Wait a minute, please, Mr. Tageka," Mannichon said hoarsely. "Do you mean to say you are going to experiment on living human beings? Maybe kill them?"

"Crock," Tageka Kyh said, "you brought this fellow in on this. You handle him."

"Flox," Crockett said with evident irritation, "it boils down to this—are you a scientist or aren't you a scientist?"

Tageka Kyh was already dialing San Francisco.

• • •

"Let me see, now," Ludwig Qvelch was saying, "what have we got on hand? I'm thinking of the Blumstein wing. That would seem to be the place to begin, don't you agree, Tageka?"

Tageka Kyh nodded. "The Blumstein wing. Ideal," he said.

Qvelch had arrived only 14 hours after the call to San Francisco. He had closeted himself with Tageka Kyh and Crockett all afternoon and evening. It was midnight now and Mannichon had been admitted to the conference, which was taking place in the Cape Cod living room. Ludwig Qvelch was a huge, tall man, with wonderful white teeth and a hearty Western manner. He wore $300 suits with light ties and he was a man you would instinctively trust anywhere. He had made some marvelously eloquent speeches on national television against Medicare.

Qvelch took out a small black alligator notebook and thumbed through it. "At the moment," he said, "we have thirty-three Caucasians, twelve Negroes, three indeterminate, one Hindu, one Berber and seven Orientals, six presumably of Chinese extraction, one definitely Japanese. All male, of course." He laughed heartily at this allusion to his specialty, the prostate gland. "I would call that a fair enough sampling, wouldn't you?"

"It'll do," Tageka Kyh said.

"All terminal?" Crockett asked.

"I would say roughly eighty percent," Qvelch said. "Why do you ask?"

"For *his* sake." Crockett gestured toward Mannichon. "He was worried."

"I'm glad to see that the rarefied air of research hasn't wiped out your admirable youthful scruples," Qvelch said, putting a large Western hand on Mannichon's shoulder. "Have no fear. No life will be shortened—appreciably."

"Thanks, doctor," Mannichon mumbled.

Qvelch looked at his watch. "Well, I've got to be

tootling back," he said. "I'll keep in touch." He put a liter bottle, usually reserved for carrying volatile acids and encased in lead, into his valise. "You'll be hearing from me." He started briskly toward the door, Tageka Kyh accompanying him. Qvelch stopped before he reached the door. "What is it again? One quarter of all proceeds to each partner, with Guatemala and Costa Rica exclusive to Kyh and Mannichon's share of northern Europe for ten years . . . ?"

"It's all in the memorandum I gave you this afternoon," Tageka Kyh said.

"Yes, of course," Qvelch said. "I just wanted to be able to clear up any little points with my lawyers when the incorporation papers come through. Nice meeting you fellers." He waved to Crockett and Mannichon and was gone.

"I'm afraid we'll have to break it up early tonight, pardners," Tageka Kyh said. "I have some work to do."

Mannichon went right home, looking forward to his first good night's sleep in months. His wife was out playing bridge, so he should have been able to sleep like a baby; but for some reason, he couldn't close his eyes until dawn.

• • •

"Qvelch called this afternoon," Tageka Kyh said. "He reports results."

Mannichon's eyelids began to twitch in little spasms and he found that his lungs had suddenly begun to reject air. "Do you mind if I sit down?" he said. He had just rung the bell of Tageka's apartment and Tageka himself had come to the door. Supporting himself with his hands against the wall, he made his way into the living room and sat unsteadily in a captain's chair. Crockett was sprawled on the couch, a glass of whiskey on his breastbone. Mannichon couldn't tell from the expression on Crockett's face whether he was sad or happy or drunk.

Tageka followed Mannichon into the room. "Can I get you anything?" Tageka asked, being a host. "A beer? A juice?"

"Nothing, thank you," Mannichon said. This was the first time since they had met that Tageka had been polite to him. He was being prepared for something horrible, he was sure. "What did Dr. Qvelch have to say?"

"He asked to be remembered to you," Tageka said, sitting between Crockett and Mannichon on a cobbler's bench and taking in a hole on the chased-silver buckle of the belt of his jeans.

"What else?" Mannichon asked.

"The first experiment has been concluded. Qvelch himself administered the solution epidermally to eight subjects, five white, two black and one yellow. Seven of the subjects have registered no reaction. The autopsy on the eighth——"

"Autopsy!" Mannichon's lungs were rejecting air in jets. "We've killed a man!"

"Oh, be reasonable, Flox." It was Crockett talking, wearily, the whiskey glass going up and down evenly on his chest. "It happened in San Francisco. Two thousand miles away from here."

"But it's my solution. I——"

"*Our* solution, Mannichon," Tageka said evenly. "With Qvelch, we number four."

"Mine, ours, what's the difference? There's a poor dead Chinaman lying on a slab in——"

"With your temperament, Mannichon," Tageka said, "I don't understand how you happened to go into research instead of psychiatry. If you're going to do business with us, you'll have to restrain yourself."

"Business!" Mannichon staggered to his feet. "What kind of business do you call this? Killing off Chinamen with cancer in San Francisco! Boy," he said with unaccustomed irony, "if ever I heard of a money-maker, this is it."

"Do you want to listen or do you want to make an oration?" Tageka said. "I have many interesting and valuable things to tell you. But I have work to do and I can't waste my time. That's better. Sit down."

Mannichon sat down.

"And stay down," Crockett said.

"The autopsy, as I was saying," Tageka went on, "indicated that the subject died a natural death. No traces of any unusual matter in any of the organs. Death occurred quietly, due, by inference, to a secondary flash reaction to cancerous material in the region of the prostate gland. We know better, of course."

"I'm a murderer," Mannichon said, putting his head between his hands.

"I really can't tolerate language like that in my house, Crock," Tageka said. "Perhaps we had better let him disassociate."

"If you want to go back to Detergents and Solvents, Flox," Crockett said without moving from the couch, "you know where the door is."

"That's exactly what I want to do," Mannichon said. He stood up and started toward the door.

"You're walking out on the best part of a million dollars, man," Crockett said calmly.

Mannichon stopped walking toward the door. He turned. He went back to the captain's chair. He sat down. "I might as well hear the worst," he said.

"I was down in Washington three days ago," Crockett said. "I dropped in on an old friend, Simon Bunswanger. I went to school with him at Boston Latin.

You haven't heard of him. Nobody's heard of him. He's in the CIA. Big man in the CIA. Big, *big* man. I gave him a little rundown on our project. He was titillated. He promised to call a meeting of some of the boys in his shop for briefing and proposals." Crockett looked at his watch. "He's due here any minute."

"The CIA?" Mannichon now felt completely adrift. "What'd you do that for? They'll put us all in jail."

"Quite the opposite," Crockett said. "Quite the opposite. I'll bet you two alexanders he comes in here with a nice, fat proposition. . . ."

"For what?" Mannichon asked. Now he was sure that all those companies and all that lack of sleep had made irreparable inroads on Crockett's reason. "What would they want with the Mannichon solution?"

"Remember the first day you came to me, Flox?" Crockett got to his feet. He was in his socks and he padded over to the bar to pour a fresh drink. "I said, we answer one question, we clean up. Remember that?"

"More or less," Mannichon said.

"Do you remember what that one question was?" Crockett said, drinking, sounding liquid. "I'll refresh your little old memory cells, reactivate the old nerve patterns. The question was, 'What the hell is yellow that we are overrun with, like rabbits in Australia?' Remember that?"

"Yes," Mannichon said. "But what has the CIA got to . . . ?"

"The CIA, man," said Crockett, "knows exactly what is yellow and what we are overrun with." He paused, dropped a piece of ice into his drink and stirred with his finger. "Chinamen, man."

The doorbell rang. "That must be Bunswanger," Crockett said. "I'll go."

"This is the last time I'll do any work with anybody

like you, Mannichon," Tageka said icily. "You're psychically unstable."

Crockett came back into the room with a man who looked as though he could have made a good living as a female impersonator in the old days of vaudeville. He was willowy and had fine blond hair and a small bow mouth and a blushing complexion.

"Si," Crockett said, "I want you to meet my partners." He introduced Tageka, who bowed, and Mannichon, who couldn't look into Bunswanger's eyes as they shook hands. Bunswanger's grip was not that of a female impersonator.

"I'll have a Jack Daniel's, Crock," Bunswanger said. It must have been the campus drink at old Boston Latin. Bunswanger had a voice that reminded Mannichon of Carborundum.

Glass in hand, Bunswanger sat on one of the scrubbed pine tables, his legs crossed in a fetching manner. "Well, the boys in the shop think you fellows have done a dandy little piece of creative research," Bunswanger began. "We had some tests run and they bear your papers out one hundred percent. Did you hear from Qvelch?"

"This afternoon," Tageka said. "Results positive."

Bunswanger nodded. "The boys in the shop said they would be. Well, no use beating around the bush. We want it. The solution. We've already set up preliminary target zones. The source of the Yangtze, three or four lakes in the north, two of the tributaries of the Yellow River, places like that. You don't happen to have a map of China handy, do you?"

"Sorry," said Tageka.

"Pity," Bunswanger said. "It would clear up the picture for you fellows." He looked around. "Nice place you have here. You'd be surprised what they ask for a decent place to live in Washington. Of course, the Russians will help us. We've sounded them out already. Makes it more comfy, reduces the risks. That long border with Siberia and all those delegations. Of course, that's the beauty of the stuff. No bang. We've been searching for something without a bang for years. Nothing satisfactory's come up, until this. Did you fellows test all the way down? I didn't see it in your papers. I was in a hurry, of course, but I wondered."

"Test what down?" Mannichon asked.

"Flox," Crockett said wearily.

"Mannichon," Tageka said warningly.

"Down to effective reaction at lowest possible percentage of solution in H Two O," Bunswanger said.

"We didn't push to the limit, Si," Crockett said. "We only worked nights."

"Amazing efficiency," Bunswanger said. He took a delicate sip of his whiskey. "We ran a few trials. One two-billionth of a part in fresh water. One three-billionth of a part in salt water." He laughed, sounding girlish, remembering something. "There's a curious side effect. It cures jaundice. You could set up a company, pharmaceutical only, and make a wad just on that. Only on a doctor's prescription, of course. You'd have to make sure nobody used it on Orientals or there'd be hell to pay. Well, just a detail. Now"—he uncrossed his legs—"practical matters. We'll pay you two million cold for it. Out of unvouchered funds. So you don't have to pay the tax boys anything on it. No record. Nothing in writing. It's a great shop to do business for. No niggling."

Mannichon was panting again.

"Are you all right, sir?" Bunswanger asked, real concern in his voice.

"Fine," Mannichon said, continuing to pant.

"Of course," Bunswanger said, still looking concernedly at Mannichon, "if we ever use it, it swings over on a royalty basis. But we can't guarantee that it will ever go operational. Though the way things look right now. . . ." He left the sentence unfinished.

Mannichon thought of Ferrari after Ferrari, dozens of girls in off-mauve pants.

"One more little thing and I'm off," Bunswanger said. "I have a visit to make in Venezuela tomorrow. Hear this," his voice was as precise as a gun sight. "I'm in for twenty percent. One fifth. For services rendered." He looked around.

Crockett nodded.

Tageka nodded.

Mannichon nodded, slowly.

"I'm off to Caracas," Bunswanger said gaily. He finished his drink. They shook hands all round. "There'll be a fellow here in the morning," Bunswanger said, "with the loot. In cash, naturally. What time will be convenient?"

"Six A.M.," Tageka said.

"Done and done," Bunswanger said, making a quick entry in a small alligator-bound notebook. "Glad you dropped in the other day, Crock. Don't bother seeing me to the door." And he was gone.

There was little more to be done. Since they were going to be paid in cash, they had to figure out what compensation Tageka was to get for his Caribbean rights and his ten-year share of Mannichon's portion of the rights for northern Europe. It didn't take long. Tageka Kyh was just as good a mathematician as a pathologist.

Crockett and Mannichon left the apartment together. Crockett had a date at a bar nearby with Mr. Paulson's third and present wife and he was in a hurry to be off. "So long, Flox," he said as he got into his Lancia. "Not a bad day's work." He was humming as he spurted off.

Mannichon got into the Plymouth. He sat there for a while, trying to decide what to do first. He finally decided that first things came first. He drove home at 60 miles an hour to tell Mrs. Mannichon he was going to get a divorce.

• • •

Up in the apartment, Tageka was sitting on the cobbler's bench, making neat ideograms with a brush and ink on a scratch pad. After a while, he pressed a buzzer. The Negro butler came in, dressed in his yellow striped vest and white shirt sleeves with heavy gold cuff links.

"James," Tageka Kyh said to the butler, "tomorrow I want you to order five hundred grams each of dioxotetramercphenoferrogene 14, 15 and 17. And five hundred pink mice. No—on second thought, better make it a thousand."

"Yes, sir," said James.

"Oh, and James"—Tageka Kyh waved the brush negligently at the butler—"will you be good enough to put in a call to the Japanese embassy in Washington. I'll speak to the ambassador personally."

"Yes, sir," James said and picked up the phone.

The Dark Music/charles beaumont

It was not a path at all but a dry white river of shells, washed clean by the hot summer rain and swept by the winds that came across the gulf—a million crushed white shells, spread quietly over the cold Alabama earth, for the feet of Miss Lydia Maple.

She'd never seen the place before. She'd never been told of it. It couldn't have been purposeful, her stopping the bus at the unmarked turn, pausing, then inching down the narrow path and stopping again at the tree-formed arch; on the other hand, it certainly was not impulse. She had years ago recognized impulse for what it was: an animal thing. And, as she was proud to say, Miss Maple did not choose to think of herself as an animal.

Perhaps it was this: By its virginal nature, the area promised much in the way of specimens. Frogs would be here, and insects, and if they were lucky, a few garden snakes for the bolder lads.

In any case, Miss Maple was well satisfied. And if one could judge from their excited murmurings, which filtered through the thickness of trees, so were the students.

She smiled. Leaning against the elm, now, with all the forest fragrance rising to her nostrils and the clean gulf breeze cooling her, she was suddenly very glad indeed that she had selected today for the field trip. Otherwise, she would be at this moment seated in the chalky heat of the classroom. And she would be reminded again of the whole nasty business, made to defend her stand against the clucking tongues, or to suppose there was nothing to defend. The newspapers were not difficult to ignore, but it was impossible to shut away the attitude of her colleagues; and—no, one must not dwell on it. She looked at the shredded lace of sunlight.

It was a lovely spot. Not a single beer can, not a bottle nor a cellophane wrapper nor even a cigarette to suggest that human beings had ever been here before. It was—*pure*.

In a way, Miss Maple liked to think of herself in similar terms. She believed in purity, and had her own definition of the word. Of course she realized—how could she doubt it now?—she might be an outmoded and slightly incongruous figure in this day and age, but that was all right. She took pride in the distinction. And to Mr. Owen Tracy's remark that hers was the only biology class in the world where one would hear nothing to discourage the idea of the stork, she had responded as though to a great compliment. The Lord could testify, it hadn't been easy! How many, she wondered, would have fought as valiantly as she to protect the town's children from the most pernicious and evil encroachment of them all?

Sex education, indeed!

By all means, let us kill every last lovely dream; let us destroy the only trace of goodness and innocence in this wretched, guilty world! Miss Maple twitched, vaguely aware that she was dozing. The word *sex* jarred her toward wakefulness, but *purity* pulled her back again.

A sound brushed her ear, something apart from the shrillings of the forest's invisible creatures. She opened her eyes, watched a fat wren on a pipestem twig, and settled to the half sleep—deciding to think awhile now about Mr. Hennig and Sally Barnes. They had been meeting secretly after three o'clock, Miss Maple knew. She'd waited, though, and taken her time, and then struck. And she'd caught them, in the basement, doing those unspeakable things. Mr. Hennig would not be teaching school for a while now.

She stretched, almost invisible against the leafy floor. The mouse-colored dress covered her like an embarrassed hand, concealing, not too successfully, the rounded hills of her breasts, keeping the secret of her slender waist and full hips, trailing down below the white and shapely legs, down to the plain black leather shoes. Her face was pale and naked, but the lips were large and moist and the cheekbones high. Miss Maple did her best: She fought her body and her face every morning, but she was not victorious. In spite of it all, she was an attractive woman.

The sound came again and woke her.

It was not the fat bird and it was not the children. It was—music. Like the music of flutes, high-pitched and mellow, sharp yet somehow—dark; and though there was a melody, she did not recognize it.

Miss Maple arose, slowly, and brushed the leaves and needles away.

Why should there be music in a lost place like this?

She turned and, without having the slightest notion why, except that the sounds were beautiful, she began to walk into the thickness. The foliage was wet, glistening dark green, and it was not long before her thin dress was soaked in many places, but she went on.

Presently she was standing in a grove. Slender saplings, spotted brown, surrounded her like the necks of restless giraffes, and beneath her feet there was soft golden grass, high and wild. But the music—which had pulsed clearly in the summer air, drawing her—was gone.

She looked in every direction, deciding to feel foolish, but somehow she could only feel disappointed. Her heart was beating entirely too fast. She saw nothing across the grove, just the surrounding dark and shadowed woods, the grass and trees and sunlight. There was the sound of the brook, of the wind, of her heart.

She sank to the ground and lay still, curiously exhausted. Then she became conscious of it, one thing which her vision might deny, and her senses, but which she felt nonetheless to be.

She was not alone.

"Yes?" The word rushed and died before it could ever leave her throat.

A rustle of leaves: small hands applauding.

"Who is it?"

A drum in her chest.

"Who is it—who's here?"

And silence.

Miss Maple put unsteady fingers to her lips and stopped breathing. I'm not alone, she thought, I'm not alone.

No.

Did someone say that? She lay on the grass trembling, and a new sensation—neither fear nor terror—washed over her, catching her up in tides.

She stiffened when she felt this, and when she heard the laughter, the deep-throated far-off laughter—was it far off?—her eyes arced over the grove.

And saw nothing.

She rose to her feet. There was a new smell in the air. A coarse animal smell like wet fur, hot and fetid, thick, heavy, rolling toward her, covering her.

She cried something inarticulate and attempted to run. When she reached the shaded dell at the end of the grove, she dropped, consumed with heat, to the softness and breathed the animal air.

Something touched her. A hand?

She threw her arms over her face. "Please!"

"Miss Maple!"

She felt her hands reaching toward the top button of her dress.

"Miss Maple! What's the matter?"

An eternal moment; then, everything sliding, melting, like a vivid dream you will not remember. Miss Maple shook her head from side to side and stared up at a boy with straw hair and wide eyes.

She pulled reality about her.

"You all right, Miss Maple?"

"Of course, William," she said. The smell was gone. The music was gone. It was a dream. "I was following a snake, you see—a chicken snake, to be exact—and I almost had it, you see, when I twisted my ankle on one of the stones in the brook. That's why I called."

The boy said, "Wow."

"Unfortunately," Miss Maple continued, getting to her feet, "it escaped. You didn't happen to see it, did you, William?"

William said no, and Miss Maple pretended to hobble back to the field.

When she inquired of the students if they'd heard anything peculiar, like music, like a radio playing music, or something, they told her they hadn't, and she looked closely at them.

But they were telling the truth.

• • •

At 4:19, after grading three groups of tests, Miss Lydia Maple put on her gray cotton coat and flat black hat and started for home. She was not exactly thinking about the incident in the forest, but Owen Tracy had to speak twice. He had been waiting.

"Miss Maple. Over here!"

She stopped, turned, and approached the blue car. The principal of Overton High was smiling. He was too handsome for his job, too tall and too young, and Miss Maple resented his eyes. They traveled. "Yes, Mr. Tracy?"

"Thought maybe you'd like a lift home."

"That is very nice of you," she said, "but I enjoy walking. It isn't far."

"Well, then, how about my walking along with you?"

Miss Maple flushed. "I——"

"Like to talk with you, off the record." The tall man got out of his car, locked it.

"Not, I hope, about the same subject."

"Yes."

"I'm sorry, I have nothing further to add."

Owen Tracy fell into step. His face was still pleasant, and it was obvious that he intended to retain his good humor, his charm. "I suppose you read Ben Sugrue's piece in *The Sun-Mirror* yesterday?"

Miss Maple said, "No," perfunctorily. Sugrue was

a monster, a libertine; it was he who had started the campaign, whose gross libidinous whispers had first swept the town.

"It refers to Overton High as a medieval fortress."

"Indeed? Well," Miss Maple said, "perhaps that's so." She smiled delicately. "It was, I believe, a medieval fortress that saved hundreds of lives during the time of the Black Plague."

Tracy stopped a moment to light a cigarette. "Very good," he conceded. "You're an intelligent person, Lydia. Intelligent and sharp."

"Thank you."

"And that's what puzzles me. This mess over the sex-education program isn't intelligent and it isn't sharp. It's foolish. As a biology teacher, you ought to know that."

Miss Maple was silent.

"If we were an elementary school," Tracy said, "well, maybe your idea would make sense. I personally don't think so, but at least you'd have a case. In a high school, though, it's silly, and it's making a laughing-stock out of us. If I know Sugrue, he'll keep hammering until one of the national magazines picks it up. And that will be bad."

Miss Maple did not change her expression. "My stand," she said, "ought to be perfectly clear by now, Mr. Tracy. In the event it isn't, let me tell you again. There will be no sex-education program at Overton so long as I am in charge of the biology department. I consider the suggestion vile and unspeakable—and quite impractical—and I am not to be persuaded otherwise, neither by yourself, nor by that journalist, nor by the combined efforts of the faculty. Because, Mr. Tracy, I feel a responsibility toward my students. Not only to fill their minds with biological data, but to protect them, also." Her voice was even. "If you wish to take action, of course, you are at liberty to do so——"

"I wouldn't want to do that," Owen Tracy said. He seemed to be struggling with his calm.

"I think that's wise," Miss Maple said. She paused and stared at the principal.

"And what is that supposed to mean?"

"Simply that any measures to interrupt or impede my work, or force changes upon the present curriculum, will prove embarrassing, Mr. Tracy, both to yourself and to Overton." She noticed his fingers and how they were curling.

"Go on."

"I hardly think that's necessary."

"I do. Go on, please."

"I may be . . . old-fashioned . . ." she said, "but I am not stupid. Nor am I unobservant. I happen to have learned some of the facts concerning yourself and Miss Bond. . . ."

Owen Tracy's charm fled like a released animal. Anger twitched along his temples. "I see."

They looked at one another for a while; then the principal turned and started back in the opposite direction. The fire had gone out of his eyes. After a few steps, he turned again and said, "It may interest you to know that Miss Bond and I are going to be married at the end of the term."

"I wonder why," Miss Maple said and left the tall man standing in the twilight.

She felt a surge of exultation as she went up the stairs of her apartment. Of course she'd known nothing about them, only guessed; but when you think the worst of people, you're seldom disappointed. It had been true, after all. And now her position was absolutely unassailable.

She opened cans and bottles and packages and prepared her usual supper. Then, when the dishes were done, she read Richards' *Practical Criticism* until 9:00. At 9:30 she tested the doors to see that they were securely locked, drew the curtains, fastened the windows and removed her clothes, hanging them carefully in the one small closet.

The gown she chose was white cotton, chin-high and ankle-low, faintly figured with tiny fleur-de-lis. For a brief moment her naked body was exposed; then, at once, covered up again, wrapped, encased, sealed.

She lay down, quite prepared to sink gracefully into sleep. For some reason, she could not. Sleep refused to come. After a time she got up, warmed and drank some milk; still, curiously, she was wakeful.

Then she heard the music.

The pipes, the high-pitched, dancing pipes of the afternoon, so distant now that she felt perhaps she was imagining them, so real she knew she couldn't be. Perhaps the radio? She checked it; it was off. Someone else's radio? No.

Miss Maple decided to ignore the sounds and the strange feeling that was creeping upon her alone in her bed. She pressed the pillow tight against her ears and held it there.

The music grew, indescribably beautiful, melancholy, yearning. . . .

She threw off the covers and began to pace the room, hands clenched. The sounds came through the locked windows. Through the locked doors. Calling.

She remembered things, without remembering them.

She fought another minute, very hard, then surrendered. Without knowing why—except to tell herself that it was terribly stuffy in the room and that a ride in the cool night air would help her sinuses—she walked to the closet and removed her gray coat. She put it on over her nightgown. Then she opened a bureau drawer and pocketed a ring of keys, walked out the front door, down the hall, her naked feet silent upon the thick-piled carpet, and into the garage where it was dark. The music played fast, her heart beat fast, and she moaned softly when the seldom-used automobile sat cold and unresponding to her touch.

At last it came to life, and in moments she was out of town, driving faster than she had ever driven, pointed toward the wine-dark waters of the Gulf. The highway turned beneath her in a blur and sometimes, on the curves, she heard the shocked and painful cry of the tires, but it didn't matter. Nothing mattered except the music.

Though her eyes were blind, her instinct found the turnoff, and soon she was walking across the moon-white path of shells, unmindful of the thousand-razor sharpness that cut into her feet.

Now the piping was inside her. She was drawn across the path and into the field and across the field and into the trees, not feeling the cold, sharp fingers of brush tearing at her and the high wet grass soaking her and the stones daggering her flesh, feeling only the pumping of her heart and the music, calling and calling.

There! The brook was cold, but she was past it, and past the wall of foliage. And there—the grove, moon-silvered and waiting.

Miss Maple tried to pause and rest, but the music would not let her do this. Heat enveloped her. She removed the coat, tore off the tiny pearl buttons of her gown and pulled the gown over her head and threw it to the ground.

It did no good. Proper Miss Lydia Maple stood there,

while the wind lifted her hair and sent it billowing like shreds of amber silk, and felt the burning and listened to the pipes.

They were frenzied now. In front of her, in back, to the sides of her, growing louder, growing faster, and faster. She heard them deep in her blood and when her body began to sway, rhythmically, she closed her eyes and fought and found she could do nothing.

Dance! they seemed to say. *Dance tonight, Miss Maple—now. It's easy. You remember. Dance!*

She swayed and her legs moved, and soon she was taking steps over the tall grass, whirling and pirouetting.

She danced until she could dance no more; then she stopped by the first tree at the end of the grove and waited for the music to cease as she knew it would.

The forest became silent.

Miss Maple smelled the goaty animal smell and felt it coming closer; she lay against the tree and squinted her eyes, but there was nothing to see, only shadows.

She waited.

There was a laugh—a wild shriek of amusement; bull-like and heavily masculine it was, but wild as no man's laugh ever could be. And then the sweaty fur odor was upon her, and she experienced a strength about her, and there was breath against her face, hot as steam, panting, chuckling.

"Yes," she whispered, and hands touched her, hurting with fierce pain.

"Yes!" and she felt glistening muscles beneath her fingers, and a weight upon her, a shaggy, tawny weight that was neither ghost nor human nor animal, but with much heat, hot as the fires that blazed inside her.

"Yes," said Miss Maple, parting her lips. "Yes! *Yes!*"

• • •

In the days that followed, Miss Maple walked with

a new step, and there was a new light in her eyes, but only a few noticed the change. She hid it well. Owen Tracy would stare at her sometimes, and sometimes the other teachers would wonder to themselves why she should be looking so tired so much of the time. But since she did not say or do anything specifically different, it was left a small mystery.

When some of the older boys said that they had seen Miss Maple driving like a bat out of hell down the gulf highway at two in the morning, they were very quickly silenced, for such a thing was too absurd for consideration.

But all were agreed that Miss Maple certainly looked happier than she had ever been, and it was attributed to her victory over the press and the principal's wishes on the matter of sex education.

To Owen Tracy, it was a distasteful subject for conversation all the way around. He was in full agreement with the members of the school board that progress at Overton would begin only when Miss Maple was removed, but he could not say this openly. "She's a first-class teacher, gentlemen, and first-class teachers are hard to find. . . ." And furthermore, she could break Lorraine Bond's heart by spreading her vicious gossip. Which she wouldn't hesitate to do. . . .

As for Miss Maple, she adjusted magnificently to a complicated situation. She would hear the music of the pipes and go to them; yet she would never believe in them. It was all fantastic, and fantasy had no place in her life. She would awaken each morning satisfied that she had had another dream; then—wondering vaguely about the spattered mud on her leg, about the grass stains and bits of leaves and fresh twigs in her hair—she would forget it and go about her business.

She did so fiercely, almost with abandon. She had

power now. Power to scrape the scandalous barnacles away, with whatever instrument she chose.

It was on a Monday—the night of the day that she had assembled positive proof that Willie Hammacher and Rosalia Forbes were cutting classes together and stealing away to Dauphin Park, and submitted this proof and had Willie and Rosalia threatened with expulsion from school—that Miss Maple scented her body with perfumes, lay down and waited, again, for the music.

She waited, tremulous as usual, aching beneath the temporary sheets.

But the air was still.

He's late, a part of her thought, and she tried to sleep. Often she would sit up, though, certain that she had heard the sound, and once she got halfway across the room toward the closet; and sleep was impossible.

She stared at the ceiling until three A.M., listening.

Then she rose and dressed and got into her car.

She went to the grove.

She stood under the crescent moon, under the bruised sky. And heard the wind, her heart, owls high in the trees, the shifting currents of the stream—and heard the forest quiet.

"Where are you?" she whispered.

Silence.

"I'm here," she whispered.

Then, she heard the chuckling. It was cruel and hearty, without mirth.

She ran to the middle of the grove.

The laughter came from the trees to the right. She ran to it. It disappeared. It came again, from the trees to the left.

Miss Maple put her hands to her breasts and knew fear. "Don't," she said. "Please, don't." The aching and awful heat were in her. "Come to me. I want——"

You want——?

"Yes!"

What is it that you want, Miss Maple?

She looked up, feeling the hot salt tears streaming down her face, hearing the mocking voice inside her heart.

"You!" she whispered.

There was a pause; then, slowly, the effluvium drifted toward her, the thick smell of wild things, lost and dead things, things that could not exist.

Do you know what you're saying, Miss Maple?

She reached out and fancied she could touch the strong-thewed back. "I know, of course—yes, I know! Don't torture me——"

The chuckle rose from the invisible space before and around her.

Do you think it's nice for a lady to suggest such things?

"I don't care. I must have it. I need it, don't you understand?"

I understand perfectly, Miss Maple.

"Then, please!" She sank to the shadowed grass floor in the familiar dell. "Please."

You never learn, do you, Miss Maple? You come to me with your scented flesh and your cries of yes and you accept me without a qualm . . . then you go back and deny my existence and frustrate and impede my spirit.

Breath seemed to compress in her lungs; she felt she could not live another moment.

Very well. I may give you what you ask just once more. But there is a price. Are you willing to pay this price?

"Yes. Anything!"

ANTIQUUS BIBLIOPOLE

"LOVER OF OLD THINGS —
SELLER OF RARE BOOKS"
3858 24th St., San Francisco, Ca. 94114
TEL. 285-2322

DATE *11-18* 19 *76*

M _____

2 PBks—				50
		In 1		3
				53

43

Plate A

I warn you, you may regret it afterward. . . .

"I don't care."

The heavy animal odor, the rich fur smell came closer to her. *You're quite sure?*

"Yes!"

And then it was upon her, and she felt its power and its strength; one contemptuous, brutal, blinding instant and it was over. . . .

Then she was alone, and it was still but for the beating of her heart.

There was one more sound. A deep, sardonic, vengeful laugh that pierced her heart like a knife. Then it faded. And everything was suddenly very quiet.

Miss Maple looked down and became aware that she was Miss Maple, 32, teacher of biology at Overton High.

"Where are you?" she cried.

The wind was cold upon her. Her feet were cold among the grasses.

There was no one in the wood now but herself.

Miss Maple put her face against the tree and wept for the first time in many years.

• • •

She went to the grove the following night, and the night after that and the next night. But it had truly been *just once more.* What it was, or who it was, that played the pipes so sweetly in the wooded place would play no more. The music was gone. And it gave her much pain for many hours, and sleep was difficult, but there was nothing to be done.

Her body considered seeking out someone in the town, but her mind rejected the notion. What good was a man when she had been loved by a god?

In her dreams, she realized this.

The music, the dancing, the fire, the feel of strong

arms about her, and the animal smell . . . a god.

Then she forgot, and even the dreams vanished.

She went to her work with renewed vigor, applauding purity, casting out the impure, holding the Beast of Worldliness outside the gates of Overton. In her own quiet way, she had put together certain information on the conduct of principal Owen Tracy and the Lit. I teacher, Lorraine Bond, and drafted a fine plan for the dismissal of both.

And she most certainly would have carried it through if a strange thing had not happened.

It happened slowly and in small ways.

Miss Maple began to put on considerable weight. Then, although she had never cared for any form of alcoholic beverage, she desperately wanted a glass of wine.

And a plate of grass, nice green grass, would taste wonderful. . . .

She went to a physician, listened to what he had to say, swore him to secrecy, and came home. She remembered the voice in the grove—*There is a price*—and she tried to scream, but she could not scream.

She could only feel the silent terror within her. Growing.

No one ever did find out why Miss Maple moved away from Sand Hill in such a hurry, or where she went, or what happened to her afterward.

But, then, nobody cared.

Somewhere Not Far from Here/gerald kersh

When I say that where I come from is neither here nor there, I mean exactly that, for my family's place is dust and ashes. And there are 32 winds. As the Dumb Ox once said, "Neither here nor there is everywhere. You are a citizen of the world, young Martin. Cheer up!"

I have nothing but my name, Martin, and I do not rate. I never had a woman. My ambition was to grow a mustache. I never shall. In another month I should be 15 years old, but that month is not for me. Tomorrow or the day after even my name will be lost. Why should anybody remember me?

Perhaps one of my friends will manage to live until there is peace and quiet. I have never known such a time. But it may come, and somebody might say, "Those, children, were the days when we learned to throw a bomb as you learn to throw a ball. The boy Martin was there at that time, and he played the man among us men. . . ."

It may be. I hope so. You are, actually, only as you

are remembered. I did my best and I fought with the rest. I have to go now where most of my friends must be. But who will recognize poor Martin in the dark?

That night I was with the guerrillas—I was one of the free men—and Mike was leading us, a good man. There were 30 of us with him that night. We had to raid an enemy dump for dynamite, fuses, detonators. When we went through the woods, the rain beat on the leaves so that nobody could hear us. It was late when we got out of the trees and crawled up the slope. Mike cut the wire and stabbed a sentry in the throat with a broad-bladed butcher's knife. Do this right and a man's lungs fill up with blood. He dies with nothing more than a cough.

The sentry's number two came by, and the Dumb Ox killed him with a handkerchief. It is an old trick. You tie something heavy into the corner of your piece of cloth and swing it backhand about your man's neck; catch the swung end and get your knuckles into the base of his skull. I have done it myself. The principle is that if you use a noose, even of thin wire, it must go over the other man's head and he, being on the alert, will see that wire pass his eyes, and turn or duck. The Ox weighed 300 pounds. The sentry died in silence. So we crept through the gap.

Mike had figured that with any kind of luck, 15 of the 30 of us might get away. "It could be a lot worse," he said. So it could. But now the enemy seemed to be fast asleep. We were quiet, God knows; we knew how to be quiet because we had been living like worms underground. But within only a little distance of the dump, somebody sensed us. He could not have seen us. He could not have heard us. Whatever it was, he let loose a burst of machine-gun fire in our general direction.

At a sign we lay still. Nobody knew where we were, or whether we were ten or a thousand strong, until they fired a flare, a white flare, which went off in the sky with a shaky light. Under that light we must have been as easy to see as cutout silhouettes. A violet flare went up then and—believe me—it was a dream, every man with a half a dozen shadows, all dancing, as Mike threw out his hand in the sign that means *Forward*. Then we charged, muddy-bellied as wild pigs, every one of us with his machine pistol and his grenades.

You would have thought that all the guns in the world had gone off at once. As the white flare died, another went up; only some fool of an enemy fired a green one. Shooting at shadows? So they were, only they filled the air with lead in a double enfilade. Mike went forward all the time and I was the first behind him. I said it was like a dream. But it was not a bad dream. Everything was so quick and bright, you wanted it not to end. And if this is child's talk, let it be.

We cut our way into the dump. Mike threw me a case of dynamite. The Ox took it from me and put it under his arm. He was as calm as if all this had been arranged in an office. Pulling the pins with his teeth, he threw four grenades. A machine gun stopped suddenly and I heard a man screaming, "Mother! Mother!"

Mike gave me four tins of fuses and two of detonators which I could get inside my jacket. Then he caught hold of another box of those round bombs you can crack a tank with, and we ran.

I was at his elbow. All of a sudden he went down on one knee. When I saw him fall, I stood over him. He was wounded, horribly wounded, split open; a terrible sight to see. What kind of strength is it that is put into a man? Torn to pieces, how does he still go on? The rain was a kind of curtain. The next flare made a double rainbow. "Back to the bridge!" Mike said. I hesitated; I was bound to obey, but it was my duty to die with him. Then he ran—not back to where we had come from, but straight into the enemy dump. He was hit a dozen times. My head was cut by a bullet, which knocked me down but brought me to my senses. I remembered that I was carrying detonators and fuses.

So I caught up with the few who were left of us at the foot of the slope. You may say without lying that young Martin was the last out.

I was blind with blood. A green flare and a white one went off, and it was just as if the night had turned to lead. Then something cracked. I recognized the thundery noise of dynamite and the snapping of Mike's box of bombs. He had got to some of the heavy stuff, because after that the dump burst in a red and white flash. A long time later (as it seemed), there was a burning wind which sucked the breath out of our bodies, and a shower of branches, leaves and bits of metal; and the rain was mud and blood.

This is the way Mike died.

We caught our breath. There were only nine of us left now, and one of us wounded—the best of us all. His name was John. The Ox said to him, "Well, friend, you've got it good. One of you lend a hand with this box of stuff. Don't take it to heart, John—I can carry you twenty miles."

So he could have. At first sight you might have thought the Ox to be nothing but a silly-faced fat man, as broad as he was tall. You would never have made a bigger mistake in your life. He was the strongest man any of us ever saw, and he seemed to be made of a sort of tough, resilient rubber. Heavy as he was, he could move like a cat. It was impossible to tire him or wear him out. I have seen him fell a tree with a double-bitted ax, using only his left hand. His last stroke was as powerful as his first. It seemed to me there was no weight the Ox could not move. He picked John up as easily as a woman picks up a baby, and in much the same way, although John was not a little man. He kept saying, "Leave me, leave me," but the Ox took no notice of this, but cradled him in his enormous arms and carried him ahead swiftly but ever so gently. I heard him say, "Leave him, he says! Christ Jesus, for all I know we might be the last free men left in the world!"

So we might have been. There was no way of knowing otherwise.

That great downpour of rain which had curtained us when we came out had stopped. It was not going to cover our retreat. The night was clearing and there was a little new moon no bigger than a clipping from your thumbnail. After that awful bang with which Mike went out of the world, everything seemed strange and quiet, almost peaceful. You felt that your troubles were over. It was peace, as I have heard old men talk of it. In a few minutes I would find myself walking home.

But when I saw John gritting his teeth in his pain, I knew there was no such thing as home, and peace was an old man's story. It did not take much to remind me of ashes and dust and the 32 winds.

• • •

I was in the forest when the enemy came through our place. When I came back, there was nothing but dirt and darkness where the village had been. The enemy were punishing us for something somebody had done—I don't know who and I don't know what. My family had lived there a long time. Where our little house had been, there was only half a wall, smolder-

ing. Among the burnt stuff, I recognized part of the
table we had eaten at all our lives. We were clean
people. The table had been scrubbed and scoured until
the soft parts of the grain were worn away and there
was a pattern in the wood I could have recognized
anywhere, blindfold, just by feeling it. They left the
bodies unburied. I buried my father and mother, first
covering my mother with my shirt, she being stripped
naked. I put my brother between them. They had
picked him up by the heels and beaten his brains out
against the floor. He was three years old.

Yes, there was plenty to remember.

I said, "Ox, I've got fuses and detonators under my
jacket. I would have stayed with Mike if it hadn't been
for that, honest to God!"

He said, "Keep the stuff dry, then. This is no time
for heroics. For all I know, we are the last of the free
men."

This made me feel better. I said, "Mike ran into
that dump with a dozen bullets in him."

The Ox said, "He might have done worse. He might
have run away from the dump with a dozen bullets
in him."

Mike's brother Thomas spat and said, "Shut up, you
goddamn Ox."

He was a strong man, too, and a brave man, but he
would never make a leader. This, as I once heard John
say, was because he did not know how to take an order.
He liked to argue. Leaders don't argue. He could give
a command, but if he did so, you had the feeling that
he didn't really expect to be obeyed. With Mike an
order was a law; where he went, you followed.

Thomas was a good man, though. So were they all;
everyone had been through fire and water and knew
what it was to bed down in hell. John used to say that

all the best men have been to hell. As the storm proves the boat, trouble proves the man, he would say.

John was a man. He was 30 years old, well educated, a man without fear, and in battle a wildcat. When John spoke, even Mike listened. The enemy captured him once and (being short of guards) broke his leg with an iron bar so that he could not run away. They tortured him for weeks. He let them concentrate on his fingernails and all that while the bone knitted. All the time he never spoke. One dark night he crawled away and escaped.

He had suffered his share—yes, indeed—and now he was dying. He said, "Ox, Ox, put me down, I am leaving a trail of blood for anybody to follow."

We had reached a little clearing in the forest, so disguised with brush that it would take a woodsman to find it. At that, a woodsman who knew that particular part of the woods. The Ox sighed. He felt the life going out of John. He set him down on a bed of moss so that his back was supported by a tree, and said, "Better let me ease that belt a bit."

"Take it off, Ox, and keep it. Keep the knife, too. It is a good bit of steel. Keep it. I won't need it now."

The Ox took the belt and the knife in silence. Then John looked at me and took out a little leather book, and gave it to me. He said, "For you, Martin." I took it. It was, I think, some book of poetry, but it was all gummed together with blood. I said, "I will learn to read."

He smiled at this. "Now go on and leave me, friends. I am a dead man. The dead weigh heavy. Go."

We said nothing. Then the Ox said one word, "No!"

We stared at him. Nobody ever heard his voice sound like that, hard as iron. He said, "While there's life, there's hope. I carry you as long as you breathe.

The free men don't leave their kind to die."

Thomas said, "Hold it, Ox. I assume command, Mike being dead."

"By all means," the Ox said, "you are general officer in command, you are anything you like. Command. First of all, though, let me tell you what we've got to do."

He had the case of dynamite open and was handing out the sticks in bundles. "First and foremost we've got to get as much of this stuff home as we can, so we divide it equally and each carry a few pounds. Fuses and detonators—they're precious. Divide them up likewise. Stow the stuff away and we'll get going. Once we get across the footbridge, we're all right. But by now the enemy is over its little shock and after us in force. Let's go."

"I'm in command here," said Thomas.

"Sure, sure." The Ox lifted John up again. He climbed out of the hollow, light and fast, and we all followed him as if we had been in the habit of doing so all our lives. Then we were deep in the woods again. We followed him because we could see that he knew exactly what he wanted to do. Although he moved so fast, I think that if John had been a bowl filled with water to the brim, he would not have spilled a drop, he carried him so gently and steadily.

He reached the stream ahead of us. There he stopped dead. I knew that something bad had happened. Catching up with him, I saw that where we had left a swift but shallow brook the day before, there was a rushing torrent. There must have been a great cloudburst high up in the hills.

We were at the narrowest part where the little wooden bridge was. Only now there was no bridge. The flood had torn it down and tossed it away.

Between us and the other side lay 20 feet of foaming water driven by a current strong enough to whisk you away like a twig. Only a few of the piles of the bridge were standing a foot or so above the surface.

This was bad. Then, as we looked at one another, a little boy came running. He was too young for fighting, but he carried messages. He shouted above the noise of the water, "The enemy is coming. A strong force. Hide yourselves. They are no more than three miles away." Then he was gone.

Thomas said, "We must scatter and hide."

The Ox said, "Got to get this stuff across the water, friend."

"But there's no bridge!"

"Then we must build one," said the Ox.

We looked at him. We thought he had gone crazy. He said, "The enemy can't get through three miles of these woods in under an hour."

I said, not knowing what I was saying, "That's right, we must build one."

Something in my heart told me that if the Ox said we had to build a bridge, he knew how to do it, and I was ready to follow him. He winked at me.

Just then I saw two people appear on the opposite bank, an old man and a girl.

We all knew them well. The old man was the girl's grandfather, and his name was Martin, the same as mine—Grandpa Martin. He had been a farmer, once, but had lost everything. Now he was one of us. He lost his farm, he lost his son and, worst of all, he lost his granddaughter Beatrice. She was about 14, and the prettiest girl for miles around, blue-eyed and with chestnut hair, when the enemy carried her off. I am not ashamed to say that I was in love with her, the way little boys are—I being only 11 at that time. Everybody loved Bea, as she was called. But she had no eyes for anybody except John. The men laughed at her for this, in a good-natured way. Once, when he was out on a raid, I heard her saying under her breath, "Let him be wounded—but not badly—and then perhaps he will let me nurse him." For John never looked at her; for all he cared, she might have been a thousand miles or more away.

The Ox said of her, "She is a well-developed girl. In the old days she would marry well and have ten strong sons."

"You are an Ox," Thomas told him. He, too, had a weakness for old Martin's granddaughter.

But the enemy was short of pretty girls. They made her one of their women, kept her in a tent. By one means and another she got all kinds of useful information out to the free men of the woods. She had learned the Patheran, the sign writing with twigs, stones and movements of the fingers that the tramps and the gypsies used in olden times. We got her out after two years. It cost us four good men. She was worth it. But she was no longer the same Beatrice. Tall, yes, and with a shape to take your breath away. But her voice was hoarse and her eyes hard.

She said to Mike, "Let nobody touch me. Let nobody drink out of my cup or use my spoon. I am sick. And where you boys have killed your hundreds, in one month I have killed three hundred generations of the enemy—them, their wives, their sweethearts and their children. Understand?"

Thomas said, "We have no doctor and no drugs. Can't we perhaps snatch one of their doctors with his black bag?"

She laughed and said, "They haven't any drugs, either, much. As for their medical officer, I fancy he will be wondering how to cure himself."

Still, seeing her on the other side of the water, I felt strong as three men, and I shouted to the Ox, "What are we waiting for?"

Thomas said, "Talk is cheap, Ox. The enemy will be here in an hour. I vote we scatter and hide."

The Ox said, "They know we'll have come here. There wasn't any other place we could come to. The woods are too thin hereabout. We've got to get across."

Big Steve said, "Ambush 'em—fight it out!"

The Ox said, "And the dynamite, the detonators, the fuses? I am going to blow up the transportation bridge."

All the time his eyes were darting here and there. He was getting everything into one simple picture in his mind—the river, the distance, the piles, the trees and the scattered timbers of the old footbridge on the bank. The clouds were gathering. More heavy weather would break again soon.

"Axes," the Ox said. "Axes and machetes." We each carried one or the other. "And rope, rope!" Every one of us had a length of strong cord tied around his waist —generally, that is. But on this fast raid most of us had traveled light. Among us we had no more than 30 feet or so of tough cord.

"Now," the Ox said, "we want a few long light logs. Martin, take my ax. There's something I've got to do."

He picked up John and carried him up the bank. There he put him down again. It took only a second. Then he ran back, snatched away Big Steve's automatic rifle and took it to John, and said, "Have you strength enough left to watch the woods?"

"Yes."

But John was dying, his back against a tree and his knees bent up to support his wounded body. His eyes were sunk deep in black hollows, as if they had burnt their way in.

Then I forgot about him. There was wood on the bank. I picked out a young spruce that the water had carried down from the mountain. The ax was a good one. I took off the top of the tree, and it cut like cheese. Then the lower part above the roots. I may be young, but I was bred hard. Still, when I tried to lift the trunk it was too heavy for me, although I was working the way some men pray. But then the Ox was with me. He picked up the log all alone and carried it to where one of the piles of the bridge stuck out of the mud on the bank.

"The water is rising," Steve said.

Thomas said, "And the enemy is coming."

The Ox simply said, "Oh, shut up!"

I wish he were here to tell you what happened then. I know, I saw; but I was working with all my heart and soul. A man is made to work only at one thing at a time. The only people who look left and right are those who weren't there. John told me once that all the world loves a bridge. In ancient times "Bridge Builder" was one of the highest titles the Romans could offer a man. He told me that there have been steel bridges that spanned oceans. But I shall always believe that the most wonderful bridge ever built or even attempted was the bridge we started to build across that flooding stream with a few bits of line and some fallen trees, with less than an hour to spare and the enemy on our heels.

● ● ●

The Dumb Ox said to me, once, "Actually, son, my name is Clem, but I don't mind if you call me Ox."

"I suppose they call you that because you are strong and patient," I said.

"And dumb, and slow. Also, because I am always chewing on a bit of grass or a straw. I can't see the things smart people see. I'm not sensitive—a goad in the ass is about as much as I can feel. I am brainless. I know what is right and I know what is wrong, but the whys and the wherefores are not for my thick skull."

And so it seemed until there was this problem. The cleverest among us couldn't foresee a cloudburst up on the mountain. But it had happened, and nobody knew what to do about it except the Ox. Later, when there was time to talk, he said to me, "Well, we *had* to get across and keep the stuff dry. What must be done must be done, with whatever comes to hand. If you have years of time and millions of money and thousands of workmen, build with steel and concrete, and good luck to you. If you have only got a bit of rope, a few sticks and sixty minutes—do what you can with them, boy, and be thankful. There is always a way to deal with things. Despair is for the enemy. To hope on and manage yourself, that is to be one of the free men."

He seemed to have room for only one thought in his head at a time. Now it was to find a way across the water before the enemy came up. "It was all very well for Thomas to say scatter and hide," the Ox said. But, as he pointed out, there was no place to hide. Downstream were the rapids, gone wild in the flood. Upstream, water that was dangerous even on a quiet day. We had counted on going back the way we had come. But there was no more footbridge. "To stay and fight it out would have been all very well," the Ox said; we might have killed a few dozen of the enemy and then died ourselves. But we had a responsibility. Dead men carry no fuses. "The enemy would have started out with a rush," the Ox said, "but they couldn't know our woods the way we do, with all their maps and their spies. We could move fast over the trail we took. They would go slower and slower, suspecting an ambush. . . ."

He stood there scratching his head and looking about him like a workman who is being paid by the hour. "Ambush, ambush," he said, and went up the bank again to where John was watching the woods. What he did there was like this: He tied two machine pistols to two trees about 30 yards apart. He fastened a length of twine to the trigger of each, and lashed the loose ends to John's elbows, saying, all in a breath, "If you see or hear them, John, bring your elbows together. Those guns are cocked. There will be a burst in their direction from two sides."

John whispered, "And hit what?"

The Ox said, "Nobody. But they'll think the woods are full of us on two sides. When they come forward, you use your own gun."

"Yes," John said.

Then the Ox came running and showed us what we had to do. First of all we had to make fast a log to the pile at our bank. This had to be done quickly, because the pile would be under water any minute now. This log had to lie from the pile on the bank to the first pile in the stream; one of us had to crawl out and lash it down. The man who lashed down the end of the first log to the second pile would have to stand there, balancing himself like a tightrope walker and catch one end of a second tree trunk. Holding this, he would have to drag it toward him so that the farther end of the log rested on the second pile in the stream.

There is a game we used to play with tiny slivers of wood—spilikins. You pick your spilikins one by one out of a jumbled pile. Make one false move and you lost the game. Now we were playing with logs, and the game was a matter of life and death.

Let me make it clear. Here is 20 feet of white water. You must lay three tree trunks across it, supporting them on balks of rotten wood, one on each bank, sticking out of the mud, and two in mid-current. At any moment there will come a wind strong enough to blow you off the earth and a downpour of rain to swell the stream. You have three quarters of an hour, a bit of rope, and nobody to work with you on the other side but an old cripple and a girl.

As the Ox said later, "Actually, you know, you can take an interest in a problem like that. Thank God I am an odd-jobman! . . . Make no hero of me, my boy. There is nothing heroic in trying to do a job in an emergency."

I said, "Ah, but what if you hadn't?"

He said, "I should have been a bungler, don't you see, a failure. I won't be made a hero of. I don't believe in heroes—I've met too many of them. You must do what you can as well as you can. That's your duty as a free man. Son, there is only black or white—meaning, there is only one alternative to bravery, and that is cowardice. If you do less than your utmost, you are a coward. You must put into your work all God gave you. The only alternative to crossing the water would have been to stay on the wrong side of it. Which would have been wrong."

I said, "Clem, you gave us the strength to do it."

"No. You made yourselves strong. You know how you can reach into yourself and take yourself in both hands and squeeze the water out of yourself until you are nice and firm. That is what we did, kid, because we had to."

"And now it seems impossible," I said.

Clem the Ox answered, "From the impossible to

the impossible—that is the road of us free men."

Now the first thing we had to do was lay the tree I had trimmed so that its narrow end overlapped the first pile in midstream by about a foot.

This seemed simple enough in itself.

We tied a rope around the thin end and stood the log up on its butt, which we jammed hard against the pile on our side of the bank.

Four of us held the rope, keeping the log upright. Clem guided the log with his hands, saying, "Easy does it. . . . Good. . . . Good, lower away."

But then, just as the end of the log touched the other pile, there was a gust of wind and a shrieking of the water. The bank was slippery clay. One of us slid down, caught off balance by the wind, and caught at the rope to save himself.

The far end of the log to which the rope was tied fell off the pile. The current caught the free end. The log and rope were like a tremendous whip with all of us clinging with might and main to the lash. The log spun. We felt ourselves going, and let go. As the water tore the log away, Clem the Ox caught the end of the rope. He braced himself. The force of that jolt as the tree trunk tried to get away drove him into the clay almost to his knees.

I took my place behind him, gripped him about the waist and held on. The rest took the rope and hauled. We played the log, and we landed it.

Clem, pursing up his lips, said, "All right. Once again, now."

Thomas said, "This is madness."

"All together, now," said the Ox.

We tried again. This time the thin end of the log fell obediently into position. I said, "Now it wants lashing down. I am the lightest weight here. And,

I can walk a log and make a fast knot."

Clem said, "Good. But hold tight to the rope as you go." He had the loose end wound about his fist. I balanced myself and walked out. Once I slipped, but recovered myself. I lashed the log fast. A third part of the bridge was built; but a third part of our time was gone, and the water was swelling, and on the other side Grandpa Martin and Beatrice were in trouble.

They, weak as they were, were trying to do from their side what we were doing from ours. The old man was a strange one. Since he had lost his land, he had been like the walking dead. Now he looked almost young again, plastered with mud from head to foot like Adam when God made him out of red clay. His log was trimmed, and he had cut notches in it so that the rope would not slip. I saw him yelling, but could not hear him. A knuckle of rock had made a kind of breakwater where he and Beatrice were, so that the water was shallower and the current less dangerous on their side. A special strength seemed to pour into them. She took the thin end. And he the middle. Inch by inch they urged it forward. As luck would have it, they got the log to rest upon their two piles. True, there were some great iron spikes left sticking out to help them there. Still, it was a thing to wonder at. But they had not enough rope. "Your belt! Your belt!" Grandpa Martin shouted, and she unbuckled her belt and strapped it tight where the logs met.

Clem called to me in his great lowing voice, "Stay where you are and lend a hand"—for he had another log prepared, long enough to reach from the second pile to the third and so link everything together.

Clem sat down upon the log we had already laid, straddling it with his legs; using his hands, he climbed a little way out. Halfway along he made a sign. The others pushed out the new log. He gripped it tightly and slid it toward me. I dragged it in my direction, caught the end, steadied it, and pushed it toward Beatrice. She and the old man got it into place.

I went back to join Clem and the others.

Then something heartbreaking happened: A rotten old miserable weeping-willow tree came drifting down. It touched a swirl in the current so that the water closed about it like a hand, swung it like a club—a very heavy club, slow to lift, quick to drop—and struck the second log at the thin end. So the middle span of our bridge snapped like a match, and the two pieces of it went bobbing away with the willow.

From the distance came a popping of shots. I looked from face to face. Now the strength was going out of us. Our last hope had gone with that log, it seemed. We all looked at Clem. Thomas said—and he sounded almost cheerful, "So now it's to be scatter and *sauve qui peut.*"

Clem's face set like stone. He said, "Easy does it. I don't scatter. Somebody give me an ax."

He wanted another tree. The tree nearest to the bank was nearly two feet thick. Clem went for it at hip level. I ran to help him, but he ordered me back. We knew why. He had won prizes felling timber in contests, using a double-headed ax in competition with champions. In less time than it takes me to tell you this, the tree was down. He had dropped it just where he wanted it to lie. Then he and the rest of us were on that fallen tree like madmen, taking off the top and the branches.

"She's too heavy," Thomas said, panting for breath. "Those other two logs will be off the piles any moment. And we are out of rope——"

Some stray bullets were whistling high overhead now. Clem said, "So take off your belts, take off your pants. . . ." He seemed to change all in a second. I have never seen such a face or heard such a voice as he said, "What? Be beat by this puddle?" We were more afraid of him at that moment than of any kind of death or disaster. He screamed like a horse in a fire. His eyes were red. He lifted the heavy end of the tree in his bare hands, alone. The seams of his leather jacket burst. Black veins swelled in his neck and arms. It was as much as the rest of us could do, working together, to lift the lighter end of the tree.

Then Clem, his legs wide apart, walked backward into the water. He said, later, that it was only the great weight he was carrying that anchored him against the current while his feet found firm places to stand upon. He was in the stream up to his waist. Then the water was up to his chin. His knees bent. The water was over his head. He was putting all he had—much more than he had dreamed he ever had—into one last awful effort. His legs straightened and he held the log above his head for just a second. Then the butt end of it was on the third pile, our end was in place, and Clem was back among us with blood running from his nose and mouth.

He told me later, "I put into one minute the strength of five years of life."

Now Beatrice was across. She had lost her boots and her trousers. "Where is John?" she asked.

Clem gave her a parcel of fuses and detonators and said, "Take these across."

"But John?"

"Take these across."

She nodded, took the parcel and stepped on the first log. She walked like somebody in a dream, crossed the middle log and then the third. She was over.

Then Clem gave me a parcel and told me to go. I went. One by one the others followed. The firing was close now. I heard John's fixed machine pistols firing wildly into the bushes. Then his own weapon, in little careful bursts. There were four or five wet thuds as some grenades exploded. Clem stood, wiping his bloody mouth on the back of his hand. I saw him sigh. Then he crossed our poor little bridge and was with us, just as the enemy appeared on the bank we had just left. It was broad daylight now.

We opened fire. Only Clem the Ox did not take cover. He took out the knife John had given him and stooped, and slashed at the cord holding the log the girl and the old man had got into position. It rolled away as the water pushed and sucked at it. With it went the other two logs. They seemed to wave us goodbye and danced away. I think I know what was in his heart just then. Fastening those three sticks together was great work.

Beatrice said to me, "John is dead?"

I said, "Yes, but he thought of you, and he told me to give you this." I took from round my neck where I had hung it the little bloodstained book with the bullet hole, and although it was the most precious thing I had—or because it was—I gave it to her. And although the free people never lie except to the enemy, I said, "He sent it to you with love."

She said, taking the book, "And this is his blood?"

"That hole is where the bullet went through. He had only two things, his knife and that book. He gave Clem his knife, but, 'The book is for Beatrice with my love.'"

She asked, "And nothing for you, Martin?"

"He smiled at me," was all I could say.

Then I had to turn away. Clem, who had sharp ears and had heard what I said, patted my shoulder with his torn right hand and said, "Well done, kid. Spoken like a free man!" Then he unbuckled John's knife and gave it to me, saying, "This is for you. I've got a knife of my own."

Thomas said, "Well, let's get going."

"Quite right," said Clem, "you're in command."

So we got the fuses and stuff to wreck Bridge K16. There, five of us died and I got the wound I am going to die of pretty soon. This is the end of *my* story.

The Investor/bruce jay friedman

S ince there were no open beds at the hospital when he arrived, the man had been put temporarily in a room used for storing defective bottle caps. Seven days after his admission, he lay there among the caps, his eyes bulging sightlessly at the ceiling. A bowl of Spanish shawl fish stood on the table beside him with a note against it that said, "Your favorites, from Mumsy." Four doctors conferred in low voices around him and when the specialist from Rochester arrived, they broke their circle to help him off with his coat. The specialist was a neat man with little feet, given to clasping his hands behind his back, rocking on his heels, making smacking sounds with his lips and staring off over people's shoulders. No sooner did he have his coat off than he was rocking and smacking away, his glance shooting out of the room into the glare of midday sun.

"I'll tell you frankly," the resident doctor said to him, "I didn't want to go out of the house." He was a nervous, middle-aged man, not technically bald but with patches of hair scattered carelessly about his head. "We've done a pile of work on him, and I say if you don't have a specialist in the house, you're not a hospital. But it *is* a baffler and everyone kept saying bring in Rochester and I do agree you get freshness when you go outside. Keep going outside, though, and you're not a hospital. In any case, the house has done it all, Doctor. Blood, intestines, heart, neurological. We don't get a sign of anything. Come over and have a look at the bugger. He hasn't moved a muscle in a week."

"Not just yet," said the specialist, rocking and smacking, his eyes high, glancing off tops of heads now so that the resident doctor found himself looking into the specialist's neck.

"I've heard that you don't look at patients immediately in Rochester," said the resident doctor. "We dart right over to them here. Oh, well, I guess that's why one goes out of the house."

"Nourishment?" asked the specialist between smacks.

"Yes, I know you're big on that in Rochester," said the resident. "A few nibbles of an American-cheese sandwich now and then. That's all he's taken. We thought we'd go intravenous tomorrow."

"Pulse?"

"Fairly normal," said the resident. "I like your reasoning. I have to confess there was a time I wanted very much to practice in Rochester. Still, I feel this is a sound house we have here."

"The patient's temperature?" asked the specialist, looking directly overhead now, as though annoyed by a helicopter.

"Irregular. It's 101⅞ just now. The house is using the new electronic thermometers. They're awfully good, get you all the way from twenty-five to one hundred fifty degrees, and they work in eighths. We're fussy about temperature and record every fluctuation. It's a program the house is developing—Snub Pulse, Study Fever. It's our pet around here, and we thought we might even interest Rochester in converting."

"What was it yesterday?"

"Let me see . . ." said the resident, studying a chart. "It was 103⅝; down around two points today."

"And the day before?"

"One hundred even," said the resident.

"Tell me," said the specialist, lowering his eyes slightly for the first time since his arrival, "was it by any chance in the nineties the day previous?"

"Ninety-nine and three eighths," said the resident.

The specialist stopped rocking and his eyes met the resident's full this time. "It held steady at that figure three days before that, didn't it?"

"Why, yes," said the resident. "Right on the button four straight days. You're good. Funny, you think you've got something down pat, temperatures, for example, and far away in another house, there's someone running circles around you. Excellent show, Doctor. You've got to go out of the house now and then, you really do."

"Plimpton Rocket Fuels," said the specialist, his eyes wide now, his mouth open.

"Fuels?" said the resident. "Are they a hive? I didn't see any sense to skin work since the whole thing's so up in the air, so I just skipped right over it. Our house dermatologist checked him, though, and found his skin clear."

"Electronics," said the specialist, beginning a slow rock of deep concentration.

"I'm surprised you buy that theory up in Rochester," said the resident. "Why, the radiation level is so low here in Queens, it would take——"

"You don't understand," said the specialist. "Electronics. Electronics stock. I'm in it. For seven days your patient's fever chart has followed the exact pattern of Plimpton Rocket Fuels, which closed at 101⅞ today. I know because I called my broker and asked him whether I should stay in."

"I don't know what to do about a thing like that," said the resident. "You think it's mental, eh? I tell you, if it's psycho, we shoo them right on. We're a good house, but we're a small house and we're not equipped to do head people."

"It's a glamor issue, too," said the specialist, peering at the sun. "That means wide swings. Christ, if only he'd been on a good, solid blue chip. All right, I'll have a look at him."

The patient was a neutral-looking man who might have played hotel-clerk parts in movies. The specialist took his wrist and rocked back and forth with it a few times, as though trying to lead him from the bed into a tango.

"Of course you see more of these in Rochester than we do," said the resident, "but it seems to me all he has to do is liquidate his holdings. Such a man has no business in the market."

The specialist passed his hand over the man's eyes and the resident said, "I don't know, sometimes I feel by your silence you're rapping the house. I'll stack it up against any house its size on the Eastern seaboard."

The specialist kneeled now and whispered to the patient. "Are you in Plimpton?"

The patient was silent.

"How many shares of Plimpton do you own?" the specialist whispered.

The patient continued to stare goldfishlike at the ceiling, but then his hands fluttered.

"Pencil and paper," said the specialist.

"We've got everything," said the resident, diving into the bedside table. The patient's hands took the equipment and in a weak scrawl wrote:

> Stock market not for our kind. Drummed into me from childhood. Work too hard for our money. Had a thousand, wanted to put it into Idaho Chips. Remembered Mom's words. Not for our kind. Would have been rich. Once lost a hundred on cotton futures. But no stocks. Thanks for your interest. Jerry.

"But why Plimpton?" the specialist said to the window, crumpling the note. "Of all issues to get on. Gorch Gas and we'd have a chance. All right, it won't affect anything, but try to get some liquids into him. There won't be any till the board opens tomorrow, but keep me informed as to any changes in temperature."

"We check temps every twelve minutes around the clock," said the resident doctor. "You'll have to twist our arms to get a pulse reading from us, but we're champs at temps."

• • •

The specialist visited the patient at four in the afternoon the following day. "I know, I know," he said to the resident, "she jumped two and three eighths today. That stock will give you fits. If you think that's a swing, watch it for a while. You've got to be out of your mind to stay with Plimpton. Still, it's exciting, a crap game every day. Tell me, did he go with it?"

"Right to the fraction. You remember, the stock opened a little soft and he was up taking applesauce. But that wave of late-afternoon buying finished him right off. I've got him in ice packs now. I was up all night with our temps and the Dow Jones index. I thought there might be some more of this. The house is terribly sensitive about epidemics. I came up with an ulcer patient in the ward who was on Atlas Paper Products for three days, but I checked the market today. Atlas went off four even and our ulcer man closed at 103½. So I guess the Plimpton fellow is all we've got. You must see much more of this in Rochester than we do."

"I don't want to talk about Rochester," said the specialist. "We've got a sick man and if I know Plimpton, there isn't going to be much time. If I was on one, I wouldn't want it to be Plimpton. Get his wife down here. Maybe she can tell us how this started."

The patient's wife had a vapid but pretty face and a voluptuous figure. "I guess you know your husband's hooked up to the market," said the specialist, rocking and smacking a bit, his eyes wandering off down the hallway. "So we thought we'd get you down here. Do you know of anything he had to do with the stock market that might have gotten his fever tied onto Plimpton Rocket Fuels?"

"Jerry doesn't like anything white-collar," said the woman, flouncing and rearranging her figure on the chair. "I'll give you our whole marriage. He married me 'cause I had red hair, green eyes and big boobs. He got me on the phone once by accident and we got to talking and he asked me what I looked like and I told him red hair, green eyes and big boobs. So he come right over and we got married. I don't know if he goes to the stock market. He goes to the burly a lot. He'll go to any burly, even in Pennsylvania. He says he likes the comedians but I suspect he's looking at the boobs."

"You don't feel he's ever plunged around on the big board, then?" said the specialist, still making soft, speculative smacking sounds with his lips.

"Are you making those at my things?" said the woman, gathering her Persian-lamb stole about her shoulders.

"I'm a doctor," shot back the specialist.

"Well, I don't know," said the woman. "Jerry delivers yoghurt. He's not in the union so he has to do his deliveries on the sly. He doesn't like anything white-collar. Is any of that what you mean?"

"You haven't helped us," said the specialist. "We've got a sick man."

When the woman had flounced off into the elevator, the resident said, "A house is only human. What can any house do against opposition like that?"

"She can go to beans," said the specialist. "What's Plimpton doing now, 104½? That means it's all up to the President. He's coming over at eleven tonight. You'd do just as well to drop your temps and tune in on him."

In his address, the President called for an end to spiteful silences in our relations with the Russians, and Plimpton took it on the chin to the tune of a 5¼-point plunge.

"I know, I know," said the specialist, getting out of his coat and making for the patient's bed. "His fever's broken and he feels better. Look, I've had this baby since it came on the boards at two dollars a share and if you think Plimpton is going to sit at ninety-nine, you're all wet. Did he close with it?"

"Of course," said the resident. "But something's going on in him. We've never seen anything quite like it in the house. Get your ear down on his epiglottis."

The specialist did so and said, "It's a clicking sound."

"Not unlike that of a stock-market ticker tape, wouldn't you say?"

The specialist got down again and said, "It goes tick-a-tack-tick-tick, tick-a-tack-tick-tick. Is that the way you get it?"

"More or less," said the resident. "It's certainly good for a house to get a wide variety of things. I may even suggest that we stop shooing off the psychos. What the hell."

The patient's hand fluttered and the resident dove forward with a pad.

He wrote, in bolder, somewhat less feverish strokes this time:

> No connection. Joke. Also do police sirens, fog-horns, and Chester Morris. Do you like to kid around, too? Jerry.

"I'd get plenty sore," said the specialist, "but I'm gentle to patients, cruel only to relatives and visitors."

• • •

Plimpton picked up only an eighth of a point the following day, but the specialist was grave and irritable. "The worst," he said. "I know she's holding firm in the nineties, but I heard something nasty from a gyne-cologist friend of mine. He claims Plimpton may buy Tompkin Rocket Fuels. You get a Plimpton-Tompkin merger and our friend will go up like a torch. All right, there's something bothering me and I'm doing my bit now." The specialist picked up the phone and said, "Hello, Connie; look, I want to unload Plimpton. No, I'm not crazy. I've got a patient whose temperature is on it and I've got to try to get it down. Maybe I'll come back in when this thing is resolved. All right, Conrad."

"I never thought I'd see the day when I'd let Plimp-ton soar and not soar with it," said the specialist, his eyes wandering off into a broom closet. "But you're either in the medical profession or you're not."

"I just want to say that I've never seen anything quite like that in the house," said the resident. "And I want to shake your hand and tell you that it comes not just from me but from the whole house."

"There'll be none of that," said the specialist. "Let me see, now. Put a call through to the company. I say do anything if you've got a patient who's liable to go up like a torch!"

"This is a new sound in doctoring," said the resident, putting through a call to Wyoming. The specialist grabbed it away from him, smacked his lips a few times and said, "I don't want any board of directors. Get me the company physician. That you? Look, I want to stop that Tompkin merger if I can. I've got a patient, nice lad, whose fever is hooked up to Plimpton and this merger is going to kick him way upstairs and out of business. Yes, it's my first. Heard of a clergyman whose pulse was tied up to the '51 Cardinal fielding averages, but I think that worked differently. I'm vague on it. You won't do a thing? I didn't think so, but I thought I'd give it a try."

The specialist hung up and said, "He says if he as much as opens his mouth, it's socialized medicine. I'm not sure if he's right, but I haven't time to go figuring it out. I'd better take a look at our man."

The specialist took the patient's pulse and said, "I hope he and his wife don't have any little dividends. All right. I know. That's not funny. I always did tell baddies."

A note in the patient's handwriting was affixed to his pajama lapel. It said:

What kind of a soak are you putting on me for this treatment? I forgot to ask about the soak. If

*it's steep, somebody's going to get it right in the
old craw. I don't see any point to being high-class
when you're doing biz. Yours, Jerry.*

"In our confusion, we forgot to submit a partial bill,"
said the resident.

"I don't want to talk dollars," said the specialist.
"Practice medicine. Did you see me sell my Plimpton?"

"I've seen things I've never seen before in this
house."

"I just don't want him going off like a torch," said
the specialist.

Plimpton vaulted four points early the next day on
the strength of the Tompkin merger speculation, but
the rumor was quashed early in the afternoon and the
stock settled back with a two-point gain. The patient's
wife appeared in the room and said to the specialist,
"I'm sorry I was fresh about what you did yesterday.
I figure you're in there with unhealth all day and you
can't help what kind of sounds you make with your
mouth when you see a healthy set of things. I'll have
a beer with you if you like."

"I'm trying to be a doctor," said the specialist.

"Maybe it was my fault," said the woman. "Plenty
of wives go to the burly *with* their old men. Maybe he
really did go there for the comedians. I want the old
buzzard to get better."

"He's in a good house," said the resident.

Trading was brisk the following day, and the net
result was fine for the market but unfortunate, of
course, for the patient. Rails, utilities, industrials, all
had nice gains by early afternoon. Specifically, Plimpton got right out in front by noon, racing up to 105¾,
and then the worst happened. At five in the afternoon
the specialist appeared in the hospital and did not re-

move his coat. "I don't feel up to examining him right now," he said to the resident.

"I want to say something on behalf of the whole house," said the resident.

"I know, I know," he said to the resident. "You're very kind. But perhaps if I'd sold just a day earlier. Or spread a rumor about bad management in the company. You don't think as clearly as you should when you're in the middle of one of these."

"This house has been privileged to see at work one of the finest——"

"You're very kind," said the specialist. "All right, I suppose we ought to call his kin, the wife, and get her down here."

"Once in a man's life," said the resident, "he's got to break some new ground, to do something out of his deepest heartfelt yearnings. I'd like to go back to Rochester with you, if I may."

But the specialist's eyes were off somewhere in the isotope ward. In 20 minutes, the wife was there.

"He went at three this afternoon," said the specialist. "We did everything we could, but you can't tamper with the economy. It's too powerful. It was something we couldn't anticipate. The stock got up to 105¾ and then split two for one. He didn't have a chance. When he dropped to the new price, 52⅞, we hot-toweled him and he did rally a point or two, but when the board closed for the day, it was all over. Look, I know I should hold back awhile, but I'm all keyed up and I'm blurting this right out, anyway. You're a doll and have you ever been to Rochester?"

"My mother said all doctors were *bastardos,* and we paid them in crops, the main one being asparagus spears. Are you sure you're not saying all of this because of m'boobs?"

"I'm a sensitive doctor type," said the specialist, staring off over her pompadour.

"I ought to collect up Jerry, but I'm not collecting anyone who's always hung out at the burly," said the woman, taking the specialist's arm. "I hope you're not a *bastardo*."

"Taking a bride is in the finest medical tradition," said the resident. "I'm backing you both to the hilt and will see to it that the house takes care of Jer."

With that, the specialist flew out of the hospital with the woman, pouncing upon her once in the railroad sleeper that whisked them northward and once again the same evening, minutes after they arrived at his bachelor duplex in the Rochester suburbs. He held his pounces to two daily through their one-week honeymoon, but on the eighth day of their marriage, the specialist found himself tearing home in midafternoon to institute a third, between hospital research and afternoon clinic. The couple then went to five, the doctor giving up afternoon clinic completely. It was only then he realized, at first in panic and then with mounting satisfaction, that they were on a new issue, something called Electronic Lunch, which had come on the big board almost unnoticed but seemed to be climbing swiftly, thanks to recommendations from two old-line investment services.

Ripples/ray russell

An invisible starship stood at rest near a canal. If the eye could have seen it, the sight would have been one of immense beauty, for it was a thing of harmonious circles: an outer rim, hollow and transparent, in which the crew of four lived and worked and looked out upon space and suns and exotic worlds; contained in this circle, another, the core of powerful engines whose surging, flaming energy propelled the ship across galactic distances. And all of this unseen.

Inside, the captain spoke briefly to his specialist, first class. "Your report is finished, then? We can embark?"

"Yes, sir."

"That was fast work."

"These rudimentary cultures are all very much alike. The report is simple—planet's inhabitants too primitive to comprehend our presence here, therefore suggest a return in a few millennia when the species may be more advanced and we can set up cultural and scientific exchange, trade, and so on."

The first mate drew near them. "Do you really think they're too primitive? They already have language, laws, religion. . . ."

"But no technology," said the specialist. "They couldn't possibly understand that we come from another planet, the very concept 'planet' is beyond them . . . no, no, to try to establish contact now would be traumatic for them. If we revealed ourselves—flicked off the invisibility shield—there would be . . . ramifications . . . repercussions. . . ."

"Ripples?" said the captain.

"Ripples," replied the specialist with a nod. "An apt word. Like a pebble dropped in a pond, spawning ever larger and larger and more grandiose images of its own smallness, so even an instantaneous glimpse of us and our ship could, with time and retellings, become magnified and elaborated and distorted—into something far beyond anything we could dream."

"Then let us head for home and a well-earned leave," said the captain.

The first mate added, "And a well-shaped young lady I *hope* has been pining away in solitude!"

"Ah, youth——" began the captain, but broke off as his navigator approached with a worried air. "Trouble?" the captain asked.

"Yes, sir, I'm afraid so," said the navigator.

"Serious?"

"A little. The main engine is inoperable—just as I feared."

The first mate said, "That rough landing damaged more than our pride."

"What about the auxiliary?" asked the captain.

"It will get us home, just barely, but it won't hold up under the strain of lift-off——"

"What?"

"—unless we conserve all other energy. That means switching off lights, chart banks, communications, sensors, air, invisibility shield, everything—but only for those first few vital seconds of lift-off, of course."

"Then do it."

"Yes, sir."

The specialist, alarmed, said, "Captain! Not the invisibility shield! We must not turn that off!"

"You heard the navigator. It's our only chance—and it will just be for a few seconds." He nodded to the navigator, saying, "Lift off." Then he looked out through the transparent hull at the world they would soon depart. "Primitive, you say. Well, you're the expert. But it's too bad we can't contact them now. It might have been interesting. They're so much like us, they're almost *human*."

"Well, hardly that," said the specialist, as the starship moved. "They're monofaced, and their feet are different, and they completely lack wings. But I know what you mean. . . ."

Outside, a bearded denizen of the primitive planet blinked, stared, pointed.

"Behold!" he cried to a companion. "A whirlwind! A great cloud! A fire! Men with wings and many faces! A wheel . . . in the middle of a wheel!"

"Where? What?" said his companion, turning a second too late. "I saw nothing, Ezekiel."

But, roiled by that whirlwind, the waters of the Chebar canal were a dancing spiderwork of ripples.

The Dispatcher/gerald green

I could swear that my secretary, Miss Minihan, addressed my boss as *Colonel* Carter this morning. And did I hear him say to her, "Thank you, *Corporal*"? Having just assumed my new job as quality-control manager, I don't wish to seem too inquisitive.

Our firm is only indirectly involved in defense work, which makes me even more puzzled. Yesterday, for example, I overheard a conversation between two elderly mechanics in the shop. It went:

"Old man's on the warpath again."

"Eatin' ass like it was steak."

"You know how it is. With the I. G. on his back."

"They don't frighten me. Goddamn brass. They'd strangle in their own snot if it wasn't for us."

At first I assumed the conversation was some kind of shop jargon. But now I am not so certain. What further disturbed me was that shortly after this conversation, Mr. Carter came to the assembly line to talk to these men. I could not hear the conversation, but a peculiar stiffness in the attitudes of the mechanics, a movement of their right arms, was evident.

Later I passed Carter in the corridor. He nodded at me and I suddenly felt my right arm moving toward my right temple, fingers extended and joined.

Carter smiled. "Go ahead, Dugan," he said. "It's all right, if you want to, even though we certainly don't insist on it."

I pulled my arm back to my side, feeling embarrassed and confused, and I hurried to my office. Miss Minihan had a batch of invoices for me to check. I went about my work, trying to make some sense out of the strange work habits here. In the midst of the invoices, I saw a sheet of legal-size paper, headed:

TABLE OF ORGANIZATION
UNITED APERTURES, INC.

I called my secretary. "Miss Minihan, what is this?" I asked.

"Oh, that. The administrative chart."

"But it says *Table of Organization*. That is an Army expression. It is referred to as a T/O, and that's exactly what this paper is."

"Golly, I never thought of it that way." She giggled.

When she left, I searched for my name. I was listed under *Headquarters and Headquarters Company* with the rank of first lieutenant.

Dazed, I wandered about the plant for a few minutes and entered a half-hidden men's room on a fire-stair landing. As I approached the urinal, a sign over it greeted me:

PLEASE DO NOT THROW CIGAR BUTTS
IN HERE
IT MAKES THEM SOGGY AND
HARD TO LIGHT

I knew at once that I was involved in neither a joke nor a dream nor a corporate fancy. They had gotten me back in.

• • •

My present circumstances recall a series of curious incidents in which I was involved some years ago, beginning with the appearance of the *dispatcher* at my home.

After my discharge from military service, I was living with my parents in an old Spanish-style house in West Los Angeles. I had spent four years in the Army, including overseas duty, and was discharged with the rank of sergeant. Now I had returned to my studies in business administration at the University of California at Los Angeles. I note here that I was never a perpetual griper or a guardhouse lawyer. While I was not delighted with serving in the Army, I accepted it as a duty.

One spring morning, I was unable to locate the keys of the old Ford I drove to classes. We were a family of comfortable means and had three cars: my old Ford, a new Mercury driven by my father, an accountant for one of the film studios, and my mother's Nash. (We did not think ourselves in any way unusual, because there was virtually no public transportation to be had.) Having searched the house and the car for the keys, I went to the small room above our garage to look for them there.

As I opened the screen door, I saw a man sleeping on the day bed. He was in an Army uniform. An overstuffed duffel bag was on the floor alongside him. On it was stenciled:

ESPOSITO SALVATORE ASN 32694853

My assumption was that he had been hitchhiking

in the area (men were still being discharged and transferred) and he had wandered in to catch a night's
sleep. I shook him firmly but gently.

"OK, Mac, let's hit it," I said. "Grab your socks."

The sleeper stirred. His eyes opened and he studied
me irritably. "Jesus, I just got to sleep." He muttered
something about "doing a frigging day's work without
sleep," yawned enormously and sat up in bed. As he
scratched, stretched and broke wind, I studied him.

Esposito was a squat, dark man in his early 20s. His
features were blunt—the eyes hooded and suspicious,
the mouth pouting. Black stubble covered his chin; he
needed a haircut.

"Get a good night's sleep?" I asked.

"Lousy. Couldn' find da mess hall. You da CQ?"

"You're a little confused, soldier. This is a *private*
house. I don't mind you catching some shut-eye, but
don't you think you should have asked first?"

Esposito got up and stretched. His o.d. shirt came
loose from his o.d. trousers. An o.d. undershirt peeked
through the gap. "Ain't no terlet paper in da latrine.
And dere better be a PX around, or I'll raise hell. I
may be oney a lousy corporal, but I got rights."

Was he unbalanced? Some poor dope ready for a
Section Eight discharge? I decided to be firm. "Esposito, you'd better get out of here. My father's got a bad
temper and he won't like the idea. I'm a former enlisted
man myself, so I don't mind. But you'd better clear
out now."

"I ain't goin' nowhere. I been *transferred* here."

"That's impossible. A soldier can't be transferred to
a private home."

"Ya'll shit, too, if y'eat reg'lar."

With that, he dragged the duffel bag to the bed,

undid the cord and groped in its guts. Out came a wool knit cap, half of a messtin, a cardboard stationery folder and some dirty socks. Then he located a single wrinkled sheet of mimeographed paper, which he thrust at me. "Dat's your copy, pal. File it or it'll be *your* ass."

I read it swiftly.

HOLABIRD ORDNANCE DEPOT
HOLABIRD, MARYLAND

Corporal ESPOSITO SALVATORE ASN 32694853 (NMI) Casual Detachment, 1145 Labor Supvn Co., Holabird Ordnance Depot, Holabird, Md., is transferred in rank and grade to 1125 Hampton Drive, West Los Angeles, California.

Cpl. ESPOSITO will on arrival at new post assume duties of DISPATCHER, Army Classification 562, responsible for dispatch of all vehicles, wheeled, tracked and half-tracked, at said installation.

No change of rank or pay involved. EM to draw six dollars per diem. Transfer at request and convenience of M. A. C. E., Washington, D. C.

Having at one time served as a battalion clerk, I realized that the orders were either the real thing or a perfect forgery. The language, the phrasing, the format were perfect.

As I puzzled over the sheet, Corporal Esposito seated himself at a table in the corner of the room. On it he placed a yellow pad and a few slips of carbon paper. These were *trip tickets*, standard Army forms for the use of a vehicle. Behind his ear he stuck a red pencil stub. He put his feet on the table and began to read a ragged copy of *Captain Marvel* comics.

"Just what do you think you're doing?" I protested.

"Look, Mac, I got a job to do, *you* got a job to do," he said thickly. His sullen eyes darted up from the comic book. "Anya you people wanna vehicle, you come see me foist for a trip ticket. No trip ticket, no vehicle."

At that moment I understood that Esposito was no lunatic, no practical joke, no error. He was real. He was the essential dispatcher. I knew his type, surly, slovenly, wary, a petty dictator—a wielder of power and influence. He wore exactly what you'd expect: a stained old-fashioned field jacket, the corporal's chevrons sloppily sewn to the sleeve; a sweat-marked overseas cap pushed back on his coarse black hair.

I wasn't ready to challenge him. I returned to the house and found my father eating his Bran Flakes and scowling at the *Los Angeles Times*. I told him about the intruder. My father, the late Francis James Dugan, was a short-tempered, choleric man. His reaction was what I expected.

"What are you worried about?" he asked. "I'll throw the bum out."

Esposito was smoking a foul cigar when we entered. He flicked ashes on the floor and called out, "Could use a coupla butt cans here!"

My father flew across the room and yanked the dispatcher from his chair by the lapels of his field jacket. "Beat it, you bum. Pack your bag and get out, or I'll throw you out."

Salvatore wriggled loose and backed against a wall. He did not seem frightened, merely annoyed at my father's obtuseness. Like all true dispatchers, Esposito had a snarling equanimity that never turned into genuine hate or permitted true fear.

"Hey, Mac," he appealed to me, "straighten yer old man out. Dis ain't my idea. Fa Chrissake, I'm here on orders, *orders*. Ya can't disobey orders. You seen 'em ya'self."

I took my father to the porch outside the study. "Pop, why start a fight? We'll call the police and let them handle it, OK?"

He agreed reluctantly and went back to the house. Suddenly I remembered my class at UCLA. I reentered the spare room to look for my keys. Esposito studied me narrowly. "Lookin' for somethin', soljer?"

"Car keys."

He patted the pocket of his jacket. "They're right here, Mac."

"Give them to me."

He took the keys out and jangled them tantalizingly. "Foist ya gotta ask for a trip ticket."

"Good God, this is lunacy. Give me those keys, Esposito."

"Oh, yeah?" he asked. His eyes were slits. "Who's aut'orizin' dis trip, anyway?"

"Captain Dugan of battalion public relations," I said glibly. "In the line of duty."

"Whyna hell dincha say so at foist?" He began to scrawl on the yellow pad. "Boy, you guys who go around keepin' secrets from da dispatcher. Jeez." He then ripped the carbon copy and thrust it at me with the keys. As I reached for them, he wickedly pulled his hand back. "Keep da ticket inna glove compartment and toin it in with the keys when ya get back."

I sat through my morning classes, hearing nothing, and got home before noon. My father had not gone to work. He was impatiently awaiting a call from Washington. He filled me in on what had happened. The local police had refused to throw Esposito out after looking at his mimeographed orders. A call to the Ninth Service Command at Fort Douglas was even less helpful. They said the incident would have to be explained by the War Department in Washington.

"I asked them what the hell M. A. C. E. was, but they didn't know." He frowned. "I'll get to the bottom of this."

"Pop, I hate to tell you this, but I think that guy is *real*. He's a dispatcher and he's been assigned here."

The phone rang and I listened on the kitchen extension.

"Department of Defense?" asked my father.

A woman's nasal voice responded. "Who is calling?"

"This is Francis James Dugan of West Los Angeles, California. There's a goddamn soldier assigned to my house. I want him thrown out, but nobody'll take the responsibility. Let me talk to an outfit called M. A. C. E."

"I'm sorry, but no calls are permitted to that branch."

"The hell you say. I'm a taxpayer and a member of the American Legion. There's something in the Constitution about billeting soldiers in private homes."

"You will be reimbursed for the man's subsistence."

"I don't want to be. I want him out. And what does M. A. C. E. stand for?"

"I am sorry, I cannot help you, Mr. Dugan."

"Goddamn it, you'll hear from me again! Or my congressman!"

But my father never carried out his threat. He worked long hours at the studio. My mother, a timid, retiring woman, had no stomach for conflict. As for myself, I was now convinced that Esposito was legally, actually and indisputably our dispatcher.

At first he was persistent in his efforts to make us accept his yellow trip tickets. He demanded the keys.

When we refused, he removed the rotors from the engines (an old dispatcher's ruse). When we ourselves kept keys and rotors, he locked the steering wheels. He was frantic about his mission. Soon all three of us began to accommodate him, accepting his yellow chits and returning the keys.

So he lingered, taking his meals in the spare room (he dutifully gave my mother six dollars a day), reading comic books, presumably happy in his work. But he became lax. The keys were left in the cars; he did not demand trip tickets. I confronted him one day. He was sacked out on the day bed.

"Goofing off, Sal?"

"What's it to you?"

"As one enlisted man to another, Salvatore, I'd say you are gold-bricking. Isn't somebody checking up on you?"

He looked around warily. "S'posed to be an officer come around. But he ain't showed yet. You don't rat on me, I'll let yez drive a car all ya want."

"You got a deal, Sal." He could be managed.

The Sunday after his arrival, I drove out to the valley community of Sandoval to watch an old Army friend, Eddie Chavez, play sand-lot baseball. My parents had gone to La Jolla for the weekend. Esposito had been absent since noon Saturday. No doubt he had written himself a 36-hour pass.

I arrived at Sandoval just as the game was about to begin, found a seat in the rickety grandstand—there could not have been more than 200 people present— and waved to Eddie Chavez. He was at home plate discussing ground rules with the umpire and the captain of the visiting team, the Lock City Lions.

As Eddie was about to lead the Sandoval Giants into the field, three men in Army suntans appeared, walking from the third-base line to home plate. From my seat in back of third base, I could see their rank clearly: a captain bearing a manila envelope and two sweating sergeants, each porting huge barracks bags.

"Just a minute!" the captain called. "There'll be a change in procedure today!" The umpire, Eddie and the Lock City captain stared at him. The captain extracted a sheet of mimeo paper from his envelope and gave it to the umpire.

A crowd of ballplayers gathered around and I heard expressions such as "What the hell?" "Who's this guy?" "Where do they git off?"

The captain addressed the crowd with a bullhorn. "By order of the Defense Department, I am authorized to supervise this game. The first event will be a three-legged relay. Teams line up at home plate."

I jumped from my seat and raced to home plate. The argument was raging.

"Hey, Frank!" Eddie called. "This guy says he has the right to run the game today! You was a battalion clerk. Look at his papers."

I did. Again I saw the reference to M. A. C. E. and the formal language. The captain's name was Pulsifer. It seemed an appropriate name for a physical-training officer.

"All right, all right, we haven't got all day. Get those enlisted men lined up," Captain Pulsifer cried. "Sergeant, tie their legs together."

The ballplayers lined up in a column of twos. The sergeants bustled among them, joining them, left leg of one to right leg of another, for the three-legged race.

"I'm sure we'll all enjoy this!" Captain Pulsifer shouted.

He blew his whistle—a bronze whistle on a plaited red-and-yellow lanyard, a whistle only a P.T. officer would carry—and the three-legged race began. It was a dry, hot day, and the stumbling, cursing players kicked up great clouds of dust as they hopped off to the center-field flagpole.

"Faster, faster!" shouted Captain Pulsifer. "The winning team gets to bat last!"

"They do not!" I cried, trotting alongside the captain. "The home team bats last! You can't just change the rules like that!"

"Who says I can't?" he asked icily. "The Army can do anything it wants."

I could think of no response to this, but it hardly mattered because the players refused to go on with the mad game. The crowd was booing, hissing. Pop bottles were thrown. But the captain was not through yet. Somehow—with threats, promises, frequent wavings of his orders—he got the teams to play short contests of underleg basketball relay, swat-the-baron and club-snatch. However, the games lasted only a few moments before the players stopped and began to yell again. How often I had played these same lunatic games during basic training!

"Play ball, goddamn it!" the umpire shouted. "Chavez, git your team in the field. Lock City at bat! And you, you *jerk*, git lost!"

Captain Pulsifer walked off the field. But as the Lock City lead-off man stepped to the plate, the officer ordered one of his sergeants to bring a duffel bag forward. From it the captain took an olive-drab contraption—a gas mask.

"By order of the authority invested in me by the Defense Department, this game can proceed only under these conditions—*batter, pitcher, catcher and umpire are to wear gas masks at all times.*" He then attempted to affix the mask to the batter's head. The lead-off man recoiled, the captain came after him and then the ballplayer swung his bat at the officer. The sergeants leaped to help their superior—the blow had missed by a hair—and the fans swarmed onto the field.

Eddie Chavez, the umpire and I tried to calm people down. For a moment it looked as if the crowd was ready to pull the P. T. O. and his men to pieces. As it was, they merely gave them a bum's rush across the diamond and dumped them into a weapons carrier that had been parked near the left-field foul line.

"You personnel haven't heard the last of this!" I heard Captain Pulsifer mutter through bruised lips. And they drove off. The game resumed. Most of the people around me seemed to think that the whole thing was a dumb practical joke.

I went home feeling dizzy from too much sun and queasy with uncertainties. That night I had a terrifying dream (one that has been recurring since I took my new job) and I woke up shivering. In this dream, I am back in Service and I am a permanent latrine orderly. I protest that I have had two years of college and have been a model soldier, but I am nonetheless kept on latrine duty because I am a "troublemaker." The latrine occupies all five stories of a tall building, an endless vitreous enamel nightmare, never-ending urinals, toilet bowls, sinks, a latrine so huge that it spills out into the street, crosses a road and deposits its gleaming receptacles in private homes, stores, factories. It generates and reproduces itself. It is dotted with signs reading: BLOKES WITH SHORT HORNS STAND CLOSE, THE NEXT MAN MAY HAVE HOLES IN HIS SHOES; or, FLIES SPREAD DISEASE, KEEP YOURS BUTTONED; or, WE AIM TO PLEASE, YOU AIM, TOO, PLEASE; or, PLEASE DO NOT THROW CIGAR BUTTS IN THE URINAL, IT MAKES THEM SOGGY AND HARD TO LIGHT.

I did not feel well enough to attend classes on Monday. Lingering over my coffee, I tried to piece together Salvatore Esposito, the baseball game and the mysterious initials M. A. C. E.

My mother came in from the living room—I had heard the vacuum humming—and began to mop the kitchen floor.

"Where's Serena?" I asked. It was Monday, and Serena Hastings, a Negro lady from Watts, came every Monday to give the house a cleaning.

"She called to say she can't get here," my mother replied. "If it were anyone but Serena, I'd say they'd made the story up. Something about soldiers stopping her bus and making everyone get off."

"What?"

My mother continued mopping. Nothing ever rattled her. Her mind always seemed to be elsewhere, probably in Des Moines, where she was born and raised and where all of her family still lived.

"It sounded so silly, I really didn't pay attention, and at first I thought it was as if Serena had got drunk, or a little disturbed. But knowing Serena. . . ."

"What, exactly, did she say, Mother?"

My mother paused and rested on her mop. "Well, she was on the Central Avenue bus, and it was filled, mostly with day workers like herself, and in downtown L. A. it was stopped by a soldier. He was armed and Serena knew he was an MP, because her brother was once an MP, and an officer got on and announced that the bus was being taken over for the day. He apologized and everything, but everyone had to get off."

"Then what happened?"

"Nothing. A bunch of officers got on and the bus drove off in a different direction. They put a sign or something on it—OFFICERS' CLUB or something like that. Serena gave up and took a taxi home. You know how infrequently the buses run. I really can't blame the poor girl."

"But didn't anyone protest?"

"I didn't ask. Frank, could you please take these bottles into the garage?"

As I went on this errand, I began to feel faint. I decided to visit Dr. Cyril Mandelbaum, our family physician. I had not been to Dr. Mandelbaum's since my discharge. His pink stucco house on a patched green plot off Pico Boulevard looked no better than before the War. An elderly nurse let me in and I settled into a sagging chair with a copy of the *Los Angeles Times*. There were five other people in the waiting room—a white-haired woman with a boy of about eight, a young Negro couple and a husky young man in denim work clothes.

"Dr. Mandelbaum has been delayed at the hospital," the nurse told us, "but I expect him any minute."

I paged through the *Times*, my vision blurred, my head throbbing. On the sports page, a small item drew my attention.

FUN AND GAMES AT SANDOVAL

A special program of unusual athletic contests highlighted yesterday's Inland League baseball game in which the Sandoval Giants defeated the Lock City Lions, 4–3.

Members of both squads volunteered for the amusing games, which included a three-legged race, underleg basketball relay and swat-the-baron. Sandoval was declared winner of the special pregame competition by Captain A. M. Pulsifer, United States Army, who supervised the program.

"This is the first of several such fitness programs," said Captain Pulsifer, "and we're delighted with the public acceptance. Fans and players both had a wonderful time."

I must have looked like an idiot to the other patients, shaking my head and muttering. "No, no," I mumbled, "it wasn't that way at all." How had this fiction gotten into print? Why hadn't they reported the near riot I had seen?

The newspaper slipped from my lap and I covered my eyes.

In a minute or so, the office doors opened and out stepped not Dr. Cyril Mandelbaum but two men in Army uniforms. One was a dapper first lieutenant with a yellow mustache and the caduceus on his starched collar. The other, a fat, ruddy man, was a master sergeant. Dr. Mandelbaum's perplexed nurse was trailing after them.

"But can't you wait until Dr. Mandelbaum gets here?" she asked. "This must be a mistake."

"Prepare the infirmary for sick call," the officer snapped.

"But Dr. Mandelbaum should——"

"No time. I'm under orders to take this installation over until further notice. Don't stand there, nurse." He barked at the sergeant. "Figler, tell the enlisted men to line up."

"Do they all have appointments with Dr. Mandelbaum?" she asked.

He waved a mimeographed sheet at her. "Government orders!"

I got up from my seat. "You're from M. A. C. E., aren't you?" I asked weakly.

"What business is that of yours?"

"I know a little bit about them. I was curious."

His yellow mustache quivered. "Figler, get that man's name, rank and serial number."

"Sir, I'm not sure he's in Service." Figler seemed a little confused. I guessed that these new assignments were so strange that even the personnel ordered to carry them out were puzzled from time to time. "The infirmary's ready, sir. May we start sick call?"

"Very well. Tell them to line up outside. We'll do this as fast as possible."

The lieutenant then marched into Dr. Mandelbaum's office and sat at his desk. Figler followed him in, but emerged immediately, brushing by the astounded nurse. He carried a large glass beaker containing a half-dozen thermometers. Dumbly we lined up at the office door—the woman and the boy, the two Negroes, the man in work clothes and myself. With a speed and deftness that recalled to me every sick call I had ever attended, Figler flew down the line and jammed thermometers into our mouths. He had one left over, so he put *two* in my mouth. No sooner were they in than he raced back to the head of the line and yanked them out. Obviously, it had been impossible for a reading to register in so short a time, but that did not bother him. In any case, he barely glanced at the thermometers, putting them back into the beaker, which he gave to the nurse.

"Sir!" Figler called to the officer. "Every one of these people is fit for duty. Not a sick one in the lot. We've had trouble with this outfit before."

The rugged man in denims looked appealingly to me. "What'n hell is this? Who are these jokers?"

"I'm not sure. But they're not joking."

The medical officer barely heard Figler. He was ripping pages from Dr. Mandelbaum's calendar, juggling paper clips, furiously dialing numbers and then hanging up. "Damn it, don't stand there all day! Come in! Wipe your feet before you do!"

Figler ushered the old woman and the boy to the desk. They stood there frightened. The lieutenant barked, "Well?"

"I ain't the patient," she said. "It's my grandson Rollie. He gets dizzy and vomits."

The officer shook his head and gave her a small pillbox. "Take two of these every four hours and drink plenty of liquids! Next!"

"But I ain't sick," the woman pleaded. "It's Rollie."

"We are under no obligation to treat children of enlisted personnel. This is not an overseas installation."

"It isn't any kind of installation!" I shouted.

"Pipe down, soljer," Sergeant Figler said. "The lootenant's had about enough of you. We know your type. You wanna come on sick call, you keep yer mouth shut."

"This isn't sick call!" I protested.

"That's right," said the husky man. "Where's Doc Mandelbaum?"

"Yeah, wheah the *real* doctah?" the young Negro man asked.

"What's *your* outfit, soljer?" Figler asked the Negro. "Labor battalion? One of them troublemakers?"

"Labah battalion?" He grabbed his wife's arm. "Let's git outa heah. I din't come for no sick call." They left quickly. The white-haired woman and the little boy followed them out.

"This is terrible!" the nurse wailed. "You're driving away all of Dr. Mandelbaum's patients!"

"How do you think I feel?" the medical officer shouted. "I gave up a forty-thousand-dollar-a-year practice in Newark for this crap! Next!"

The big man in denim walked to the desk. He was rubbing his fists.

"What's your problem?" the officer asked.

"None of ya friggin' business," the man said. "I done doody already. Five years combat engineers. Where's Mandelbaum? What'd you jerks do wit' him?"

Figler moved toward him. "Watch yer language, soljer."

"You call me soljer onct more, yer ass'll be suckin' wind."

"I'll handle this, Figler." The medical officer got up. His mustache bristled. "All right, you, what's your outfit?"

"I ain't tellin' you nothin'. Pill roller."

"You'll regret this," the officer said. He was trembling now.

"Chancre mechanic."

"Figler——"

"Clap surgeon. Go run a pro station."

Seething, the officer began dialing. "I'll throw the book at you!" he yelled. "You'll be up for a general court-martial! Hello, hello, operator, get me the military police!"

The rugged man yanked the phone from his hand and shoved the officer roughly. Sergeant Figler hurled himself at the man's back. Then the rear door of the office opened and Dr. Mandelbaum walked in. At that time, the doctor was in his 60s, but he was still just as strong and as fit as when he was on the USC wrestling team.

"What the hell is this?" Dr. Mandelbaum shouted. His weeping nurse tried to explain.

The lieutenant retreated to a corner of the room. The big man, seeing Dr. Mandelbaum, stopped his lunge at the officer.

"Now, then, Mandelbaum," the medical officer snapped, "we've a file on you. This mission will help all of us, including you, yourself. We are here in the national interest. That man threatened me and I'm having him brought up on charges of insubordination!" He was slightly hysterical. He was not carrying out his assignment as well as my dispatcher had.

"What are you talking about?" Dr. Mandelbaum yelled. "Who are you to bust into my office and abuse my patients? That's Al Zawatzkis. He's been my patient for years. I delivered him. He's never welshed on a bill in his life."

"Then you are prejudiced in his favor," the officer said. "I'll see to it that you aren't called to testify at his court-martial!"

He began dialing again. "I want the military police, and if you can't get them, I'll talk to the Defense Department, office called M. A. C. E.——"

Dr. Mandelbaum grabbed him by his shoulder straps and shook him as if he were a rag doll. The lieutenant screamed for help. Figler tried to pry Doc Mandelbaum loose, but big Zawatzkis thundered at him. It was no contest. He plucked Sergeant Figler from Doc and threw him against a filing cabinet. While Figler lay there stunned, Zawatzkis tried to untangle the two physicians. I have to give credit to the Army officer; he was tenacious and brave. He clung to Mandelbaum, wheezing and hissing and protesting that we were all traitors, but he was no match for Zawatzkis. The medical officer sprawled on the X-ray table, then got a second wind and came at Zawatzkis, who smashed a jug of green soap over his head.

The lieutenant hit the floor. The jug broke clean. The medic wasn't cut, merely bruised and coated with the viscous fluid. "Get him out," Doc Mandelbaum said. I gave Zawatzkis a hand. We picked up the semiconscious officer and carted him out of the office.

"He slipped!" I said loudly. "I saw it! He slipped on the floor!"

Dr. Mandelbaum helped Sergeant Figler to his feet and escorted him to the front door. "Be a nice boy, not a schlemiel," he was saying to him. "What is all this nonsense? Go get a job instead of being a bum in the Army all your life." The three of us—Doc, Zawatzkis and myself—stood on the sidewalk as Figler, crying softly, drove off in the jeep with his superior. Then we went into the office, where Doc took care of us in his usual considerate manner.

That evening at the dinner table, I kept my thoughts to myself. Esposito dropped down to pick up his dinner, greeted us sullenly and retreated to his sanctuary. We rarely saw him anymore. He had long stopped bothering us for car keys or trip tickets.

"I wish that tramp would go," my father said. It was exactly one week that Salvatore had been with us. "And I wish I knew why he's here."

"He doesn't bother anyone," my mother said. "And he is never behind with the six dollars a day."

"Who needs it?" my father grumbled.

"He keeps the room clean," my mother said defensively. "His personal appearance isn't much, but the bed is always made."

"*Bed*," my father said. "Did you tell Frank what happened at the hotel in La Jolla yesterday?"

"You mean the tennis match?"

"No, no. That business with the beds. You know, what we saw when we were going down to the pool."

"What happened?" I asked.

My father stirred his coffee. "It was either a practical joke or else they were rehearsing for a movie or something. Maybe a publicity gimmick for a movie. That old hotel has been used a lot for locations."

"Francis, you asked the manager that; he said no."

"Yeah. But if it wasn't a movie stunt, what was it?" My father shook his head.

"But what, exactly, happened?" I asked.

"Your mother and I were on our way down to the pool, when we passed this room with the door open. There was a lot of yelling going on and I peeked in. There were five people in the room—a young couple, a chambermaid and this Army officer and a sergeant. One with all those stripes up and down."

"First sergeant," I said. My hands were sweaty; a stone was growing in my stomach.

"This captain kept yelling that he was *gigging*— whatever that is—gigging the two guests because the beds weren't made with hospital corners."

"It *was* very strange," my mother said. "Like a silly motion picture, as Daddy says."

"This sergeant tried bouncing a dime off the bed-spread a few times, but it wouldn't bounce, and this got the captain sore. He also had white gloves on and I saw him run his finger through the closet shelves."

"Didn't the guests object?" I asked.

"They were scared," said my father. "I think they were honeymooners and figured somebody was kidding them. The guy kept saying the chambermaid had made the bed and the officer kept shouting, 'We want results, not excuses, in this man's Army!' Probably be a funny story in the papers about it."

I wondered, would it be a funny story like the lying account of the baseball game at Sandoval? How would they handle inspection? As a cheerful course in modern hotelkeeping?

The last incident in this sequence of events—that is, the last up to my current listing on a *Table of*

Organization as a first lieutenant—took place the very next day.

Unhearing, I sat through morning classes and decided to spend the afternoon in the library. In the interests of economy, I had been driving home for lunch (we live a few minutes from the Westwood campus), but on this day I went to the school cafeteria. I arrived a moment after it had reopened for lunch and was greeted by an odd tableau.

The five colored ladies who manned the counter were clearly upset. They were huddled away from the steaming food vats. The manager, a Mr. Sammartino, as I recall, was in front of the counter, gesticulating and appealing to—— Need I go on?

Looming behind the great aluminum bins of tunafish timbale, chicken and noodles, breaded veal cutlet and eggplant parmesan was one of the fattest men I have ever seen. He wore a filthy, sweat-stained fatigue suit with sergeant's stripes stenciled on the sleeves. On his head was a green fatigue cap, the brim upturned and stenciled with the name TEXAS. He brandished two enormous tools—a devil's fork and an ogre's ladle —and he sweat gallons into the food. A nauseating and disgusting figure, he was incontestably a mess sergeant. I needed no mimeographed orders to tell me so.

"Come and git it, fo' I throw it to the pigs!" he bellowed. "Yeah, hot today, hot today!"

He had an underling, a short, hairy man in dirty fatigues, who bustled through the kitchen doors, lugging a steaming pot of some appalling pink stew.

"Lady wit' a baby!" yelled the small man. "Hot stuff comin' through!"

"That's mah boy!" the mess sergeant beamed. "Li'l ole Hemsley. Hemsley a good ole boy. Look lak Hemsley brewed himself a mess of good ole S.O.S. Shit on a shingle! Give us a ole rebel yell, Hemsley."

Hemsley obliged. The air shivered with the sound. The Negro ladies retreated even farther back. One, a bespectacled woman of great dignity, appealed to Mr. Sammartino.

"If this a fraternity prank, Mr. S.," she said, "it gone far enough. The girls is fed up."

The manager paced feverishly. "But they said they had *orders*! They gave me *this*!" Mr. Sammartino waved a mimeographed sheet of paper. By now a queue of hungry students had formed in back of me. Most of them were amused by the insanity behind the steam table, assuming, as did the woman, that it was some form of undergraduate humor.

The mess sergeant stirred his pink S. O. S., stabbed at a gray sparerib, sniffed the okra soup. "Ole Hemsley. He a good ole boy. Hemsley, y'all got some grits back there, so's we can show the Yankees how rebels eat?"

"I wouldn't be for knowin', but I'll look."

"Well, be for lookin'."

Hemsley vanished into the kitchen, clanging empty pots, I took a clean tray and started down the line, as if drawn to some rendezvous with fate. The colored girls shrank away. The huge sergeant seemed to fill up all the space behind the counter.

He eyed me with contempt. "Y'all got a chow pass?"

"Y-yes," I stammered. "Company and company headquarters. What's for chow, Sarge?"

A grin widened his pulpy face. He was in *control*. He had me. "Fly shit 'n' brown pepper."

"That's OK," I said hoarsely. "So long as it ain't the same as what we had yesterday."

Chuckling, he began to load up my tray. A glop of

mashed potatoes landed in the middle. Two slices of bread hit next and were promptly buried beneath the horrid S. O. S. A brownish mixture of vegetables was hurled, spattering the empty spaces of the tray. Several wilted leaves of lettuce were inserted in the brown ooze; a rubbery veal cutlet came to rest in the S. O. S. There remained but two square inches of inviolate mashed potatoes. The sergeant grinned at the tray. "Looks like we kinda missed a spot, right, buddy boy?" I said nothing. I knew what was coming. He ladled out a yellow cling peach, swimming in syrup like the inside of a roc's egg. Leaning over the counter, he deftly set the peach half in the midst of the potatoes, drowning everything else in the sweet juice.

"Now you all set," he beamed.

The blood roared to my skull. I breathed deeply, glanced at the wailing manager and lifted the tray high, as if sacrificing it to a god unknown. Then I hurled it at the fat sergeant. He took the blow—stunned, soaked, steaming—a great abstract work of food. I fled to cheers and laughter.

Upon returning home, I went to the spare room. Corporal Salvatore Esposito was sacked out, reading *Famous Funnies*.

"Get going, Salvatore," I said. "I am throwing you out, right now."

"I don't go unless ya got orders for me."

"No, no, you must leave. And you tell your superiors you were thrown out, that we didn't want you and shouldn't have let you stay. The only reason you stayed so long was because of a delay in policy."

He sat up in bed. "I ain't goin' and you know it."

I walked to my father's golf bag and pulled out the driver. "Pack, soldier. I could handle you without this, but I want to make sure you leave in a hurry." I whipped the air a few times.

He struggled out of bed, a stumpy troll in droopy khaki drawers and socks. "Jeez. Din't think you was dat kind of guy." He dressed hastily, slung the bag over his shoulder and asked if he could make a telephone call. I permitted him to. He dialed swiftly, identified himself and asked that a jeep meet him at the corner, on Olympic Boulevard. I gave him his trip tickets, the carbon papers and the pencil, which he had carelessly left on the table. I wanted all traces of him obliterated. We walked to the street corner. Salvatore squatted on his sack.

"Who sent you here, Salvatore?" I asked.

"I dunno. I git assigned, I go."

"What is M. A. C. E.?"

"I dunno. All I know is someone's gonna get chewed out for throwin' me out." He glowered at me, but it was a meaningless glower, one for the record. "It'll be your ass, Dugan, not mine."

An open jeep, driven by a young second lieutenant, pulled up to us. "Spasita?" he asked.

"Dat's me." Salvatore didn't salute. He tossed his bag in the rear of the jeep and climbed in.

"Orders come through, Spasita. You transferred."

"They did not!" I shouted. "He was not transferred! I threw him out! Why was he sent to me, anyway? I never wanted him!"

The shavetail studied me innocently. "Beats me, mistah. We git orders and folla them.

"All set, Spasita?" He gunned the engine.

"Just a minute," I said. "I demand an explanation. What does M. A. C. E. mean?"

"Never heard of it." And the jeep drove off.

"Remember what I said, Salvatore!" I shouted after them. *"I threw you out! You tell them!"*

Did I imagine it? Or did my dark dispatcher turn and answer my hysterical request with a nod of his head, a wink?

· · ·

Today I sit in my air-conditioned office and think about my new job. Who decided I was first lieutenant? I have discharge papers at home showing that I was released from military service "for the convenience of the Government" some years ago. When was I commissioned? By whose authority?

I stopped Carter at the water cooler late this afternoon. My arm did not rise in salute, but he gauged the confusion on my face.

"I saw the T/O," I said. "Am I to call you Mister or Colonel?"

"It doesn't matter, Dugan," he said pleasantly. "One way or the other. We don't stand on ceremony in this outfit."

"But what are we?"

He smiled. "Little bit of everything, you might say. You'll get used to it."

We walked down the corridor together. I glanced down at his shoes—highly polished mahogany-brown officer's pumps with a strap instead of laces. They say to me: PX.

"Colonel, did you ever hear of an outfit called M. A. C. E.? Just after the War?"

"M. A. C. E.? Yes, I remember it. It was obsoleted a long time ago. We tried it out briefly. A pilot project, a really primitive one. We were just sort of fiddling around in those days."

"What did the letters stand for?"

"Military and Civilian Enterprises. Nothing mysterious about it."

"It was abandoned?"

"Naturally. We've got more sophisticated systems today. Data programing, circuitry. The whole operation is computerized. I must say, somebody in Washington is doing a marvelous job. M. A. C. E.! My goodness, I haven't thought about that old one-horse operation in years!"

He entered his office. I could hear people snapping to attention inside.

My nylon shirt is drenched; my knees are water. How did it happen? How in heaven's name did I get here? I curse Corporal Salvatore Esposito, my late dispatcher. He never told them that I threw him out. I am certain of that.

Wise Child/john wyndham

Dr. Solway folded his napkin, put it neatly beside his place and rose from the table, leaving his wife and his assistant still seated there.

"I think I'll put in an hour or two in the lab," he announced as he left the room.

"Just," said Helen Solway, "just as if he didn't always 'put in an hour or two' every evening."

The assistant looked at her for a moment, then, with a little shake of his head: "He is annoy. I think I get sack now."

Helen Solway frowned.

"Oh, no, Marcel! Not as bad as that, surely?"

"But yes, I think. We have big row this afternoon. He is much—how you say—*bouleversé*? Is not first time, you know, but is more serious."

"Oh, dear. Marcel, why can't you be more tactful with him?"

The assistant shrugged.

"Is not matter for tact—is time for truth."

"You don't mean you've lost faith in his work—in his ideas?"

"*Non, non.*" The young man's headshake was emphatic. "His ideas is good. Is proved. But zis"—he waved a comprehensive hand—"is not right *milieu,* setup, now. Is too little. No good."

He paused.

"*Aussi,*" he went on, "is not good for me—for me professional, you understand. Last month the *docteur* read a paper to the *Société.* 'Observations on the In'eritance of Acquired Abilities,' he call it. *La matière* —ze stuff—she is good. But ze manner—*mon Dieu! Maladroit*—not make them to understand what he say. They listen polite, but afterward they shake the heads and laugh. 'Is Lysenko-ism,' they say. 'Why he not go to Russia? Is crackpot.' "

Marcel paused again and shook his head sadly.

"*Le docteur* is *not* crackpot. Is clever man. Is great thing he does—very great, *formidable!* But he is *tout à fait égoïste*—you say, ver', ver' selfish. Do it 'imself. No one else. So all glory, all *éclat* is for him."

Mrs. Solway did not disagree with that. She said:

"But I thought you said he has proved his ideas, Marcel?"

"Oh, yes. Little proofs. But necessary now is big proofs—big-scale tests. Such is not possible here. With big tests they take notice. Is way of common sense.

"These things I tell 'im. 'Put your work to *Société,*' I say, 'to *Université* to make test, then you have prestige, official standing. Then they listen.' He do not like. Is not my business, he say. I say his discovery *is* my business—is every man's business. Is important, too important for small thinking. Is pity 'e do not speak French. I explain then more *gentiment*—more tactful, per'aps." He shrugged. "Or maybe not so. Anyway, so we 'ave big row. So I think I get sack."

"Oh, I am sorry, Marcel. Perhaps he will have cooled off by tomorrow."

"Me, I am sorry, too. But I do not think he cool off zis time. He is great man, your husband—also very little man. . . . *Alors.* . . ." He shrugged his shoulders. "So four, five weeks, perhaps, and I think I go away. . . ." He brooded for a moment, then his tone lightened:

"But now is enough of this. . . . Let us to talk of other things more interesting than sacks. . . ."

• • •

Dr. Solway's "hour or two" was, as usual, more nearly four, so that it was after 12 when he came upstairs. He found his wife in bed, but still with the light on, reading. He sat down on the side of the bed and started to unfasten his shoes.

"The children all right?" he inquired. "I thought I heard David cough as I came past."

"It's nothing," she told him. "Just the vestige of his cold. Not a peep out of them the whole evening." She considered him. "You're looking tired, Donald. You work too hard. You really ought to ease off."

"I am tired," he admitted. "But it's really finished— the important part of it—now. Just a matter of checking and cross-checking results so that none of my dear colleagues can pick holes in them. What I must have is evidence that is accurate, plain and indisputable. Something that *can't* be ignored—that, and the opportunity of a fair hearing. . . ."

He sat moodily swinging his shoe on a finger hooked inside the heel.

"If only I could make a start by knocking into their thick heads what I'm talking about . . ." he muttered more to himself than to her. "Every time I attempt a public explanation, it's the same old story: A lot of dimwits who've not been listening to what I've been telling them dismiss the whole thing with parrot cries of 'Lysenko! Lysenko!'—and a number of still dimmer wits rally round to congratulate me because Lysenko is a Russian, and Russians are wonderful, so he must be right; and off they launch into dissertations on the inheritance of acquired characteristics. . . . And after a bit I lose my temper and shout at them, and everyone thinks it's uproariously funny, and they go away more convinced than ever that I'm cracked. . . .

"They won't one day. I can promise them that. But in the meantime, they're all too prejudiced to give my evidence a fair hearing—damn them!"

Helen, regarding him thoughtfully, said:

"But you do have enough evidence, Donald?"

"Plenty—for a fair-minded man. The trouble is they can't clear their addled brains enough to be fair. Again and again I've explained to them that it's *not* acquired *characteristics* I'm concerned with—it's the inheritance of acquired *abilities*, which is utterly different, and they ought to have the wits to see it is. . . ."

"Well, to someone like me, it does sound like rather a fine distinction, Donald."

"They're not supposed to be someone like you, my dear. Their job is to think about such things, professionally—only they don't.

"The difference is as wide as an ocean, Helen. Look, everyone knows that if you were to amputate a mouse's right foreleg for ten, twenty, fifty generations, its offspring still would not have acquired the characteristic of being born without a right foreleg—and never would. . . . But compare the case of a bird that builds a particular kind of nest. Somewhere back along the line, its ancestors *learned* to build their nests like that, and the present bird builds nests that are absolutely the same in construction—nobody taught it; it *inherited* the ability that its ancestors had acquired.

"Very well, then, some species can do that—then why not others? Is it not utterly preposterous that while a spider can endow its offspring with the ability to construct such a complicated engineering proposition as a web, a man should not have the power to hand on to his son even the ability to do simple arithmetic? Of course it is. It was quite clear to me that there must be some way of inducing such a capacity.

"Look at the waste that's caused by lack of it! No conservation or progress. Every child having to begin exactly where its parents began; generation after generation tediously having to learn its A, B, C, and two-plus-two, and cat-sat-on-the-mat over and over again, just as if no one had ever learned it before. It's a nonsensical way of going on. It simply *can't* be more *difficult* to hand on the rudiments of reading, writing and figuring than it is for a bee to hand on the complicated social knowledge required to run a hive.

"I argued that there must be a reason why in some species the capacity to hand on an acquired ability was very strong—even though it may have ossified later—while in others it is virtually indiscernible. Do you follow me?"

"Yes, I think so, Donald. It really amounts to asking why some kinds of creatures have very, very complex instincts and others only the simplest, doesn't it?"

"Roughly, yes—though 'instinct' is a treacherous word—but it is, in effect, what I asked, and what I set out to discover. Well, I admit I've not discovered the why—though I may do so yet. But on the way I did come across something else: I found the *means* of producing a result, while still not understanding the cause.

And now I am able to show that it is possible, even with mammals, to induce the capacity to transmit an ability to the offspring. I can *prove* it with the results of a dozen experiments."

"I don't quite see—I mean, how do you prove a thing like that?" Helen asked with a frown.

"Well, one quite simple way was with rats. I taught a male rat and a female rat to find their way through a maze to reach their food. Just a simple maze at first, which I gradually made quite complicated. I practiced them until they could find their way to the food with never a false turn or a hesitation. Then I treated both of them and mated them. When the offspring were a few weeks old, I let them get hungry; then I took each in turn and set it down at the entrance to the maze. One after another, they bolted through it to get the food—not one of them took a single wrong turning. They *knew* their way, although they'd never seen the maze before. . . . Later on, I mated two of the young ones, and *their* offspring tackled the maze first shot, just as well as their parents had. Well, you see what that means?"

His wife ignored the question to put one of her own.

"You said you 'treated' the original two. How did you do that?"

"I doubt if you'd understand the details, my dear— and in any case, they're my own secret at present, but the administration is quite simple. It can be done either by direct injection or by introducing the agent into the diet—the latter is slightly preferable on account of the more gradual assimilation into the system. But you do see what it means, don't you?" he repeated.

"If it were to be applied to human beings, their child would not have to start right from the beginning like other children. He'd be born with a—a sort of built-in background. Think of the pointless drudgery that that would spare him. The rudiments, at least, of all the things we've had to learn one generation after another would be there already. He'd be able to read as soon as he was born—well, not quite that, but as soon as he had learned the physical control of his eyesight—talk as soon as he could manage his tongue, and count, too. Just think where he might get to with such a flying start over his contemporaries. School over in a few years, university by the time he was nine or ten. He'd be a wonder child. . . . And in the face of evidence like that, any doubts about the transmissibility of acquired abilities would simply be swept away. . . ."

He paused and glanced at his wife. She was regarding the open pages of her book with a curiously fixed intensity. He went on:

"One can't tell in advance, of course, to what extent actual knowledge would be transmitted. That's going to be one of the interesting things to find out. That the abilities that have become almost unconscious skills would be inherited, I have little doubt, but it *might* go further. . . . It isn't impossible that he would find himself already equipped to the extent of what we consider to be average education——"

"Oh, yes," his wife broke in unexpectedly, "and perhaps he'd be equipped with a taste for cigarettes, for sherry before dinner—and what about built-in political loyalties?" she suggested.

Dr. Solway blinked.

"Well, why not?" she demanded. "Have you any method of selecting what is to be transmitted from what is not?"

He frowned, a little put out.

"Possibly one would have to be careful," he admitted, "but I imagine that if, when one was under treatment, one took trouble to practice only those abilities that are desirable and have, as I said, become almost unconscious skills——"

"You imagine!" his wife interrupted scornfully. "Donald, you never gave a thought to the *extent* of the inheritance until now. Well, I can do some imagining, too—and the answer is 'No!' Quite definitely and comprehensively, 'No!' "

Dr. Solway blinked again.

"My dear, I don't know what you mean. . . ."

"Oh, don't *pretend*, Donald. Do you think after these years I don't know you well enough to see what you're working up to? It's a positively revolting suggestion. No man who had any respect for his wife would even think of it. I wonder you're not ashamed to make it."

"But, my dear. I've not made any suggestion. I only said——"

"Oh, it might have taken you another ten minutes or so to get round to it. But it was coming. And I must say, I never heard of anything more sordid and disgusting. Putting me, your own wife, on a level with your guinea pigs and rats. Perhaps you'd like me to go into a cage in the lab, with the rest of the experimental material. . . ."

"Now really, Helen, there's no need to take it like that. I admit I was going to ask you what you *thought* about it. . . . After all, to become world-famous: the first parents of a new race of, well, geniuses wouldn't be overstating it, I should think——"

"Indeed. Well, now you know just what *I* think— and that is that it is a shameful as well as a revolting idea. Only this evening Marcel was telling me that people are saying you're a crackpot, and I must say after hearing this, I'm not surprised."

The doctor frowned.

"Oh, so Marcel thinks——"

"No, he doesn't. Marcel believes in your work. He says you are a great man. Though what he'd say if he heard about this idea I don't know—at least, I do."

"Whatever that may mean—but since he is not likely to know about it unless you tell him, does it matter?"

"Of course! How would you like it if someone you'd promised to love, honor and obey suddenly wanted to put you in with the laboratory animals?"

"I wasn't saying that *that* didn't matter. It was about Marcel knowing—I mean, not knowing—oh, Lord, what's he got to do with it, anyway? Look, I'd no idea it would upset you like this. I thought the opportunity to take a part in the launching of a world-shaking discovery—oh, well, clearly that isn't how you see it."

"It certainly isn't. I think it's the most——"

"Yes, yes, you told me that. I can't say that I understand your point of view—after all, I would be just as much in the experiment, and I'm prepared to play my part—but, of course, if the idea doesn't appeal to you, there's no more to be said."

"Doesn't appeal, indeed! There's a whole lot more I *could* say. Never did I think——"

"My dear, I've told you I didn't mean to upset you. I'm sorry I did. I apologize for it. The whole idea was obviously a mistake. Do you think we could agree to wash it right out and forget about it?" He looked at her with such earnest appeal that she was somewhat mollified.

"Well, I don't know," she said. "It wasn't at all a nice suggestion to have made, not an easy thing to forget. But I suppose a man wouldn't properly understand. Now, if you were a woman——"

"If I were a woman, the proposition could scarcely have arisen," he pointed out.

"I dare say. But all the same. . . ."

"But you will try to consider it all unsaid?"

"I—oh, very well, I'll do my best. But really, Donald . . . !"

Later, when he had finished preparing for bed and was in the act of climbing in, she said:

"Marcel thinks you are going to dismiss him."

"Marcel is perfectly right," he told her.

"Oh, dear," she said. "And he is so much nicer than those oafs we had before. Is it just because you had a bit of a row this afternoon?"

"It is not. I employ Marcel to assist me—not to direct me. We've got to a point where we differ on a matter of policy. I can't keep him here if he is going to pull a different way all the time, so I shall tell him he can pack up at the end of next month. That'll give him nearly seven weeks to find something else. He'll not have any difficulty with that these days."

"It seems a pity. You've nothing against his work?"

"Certainly not. He's a good worker. He should do well—if he can bring himself to stop interfering in matters of policy that are not his concern. No, I've had enough of it. I'm giving him formal notice tomorrow—and there'll be a good reference if he wants one. . . ."

• • •

The weeks went by. Dr. Solway's thought of extending his experiment from the laboratorial to the domestic field took its place with other little lapses that could be forgiven, though recorded. Marcel bestirred himself to seek other jobs, and was pleased to be accepted for one in France. Helen Solway drove him to the station on the last day of the following month.

"He was quite cheerful—no hard feelings at all," she reported. "I think he's happy at the prospect of getting home again. I doubt whether he would ever have settled properly here. He says it makes him tired trying to express himself in English—or what he thinks is English—and he doesn't like English weather, or tea, and he doesn't think English food has been suiting him, so what with one thing and another——" She broke off as she caught a sudden expression on her husband's face. "Oh, he was quite nice about it— nothing personal. After all, a lot of people who've been brought up all their lives on one kind of food do find it difficult to get used to another. Plenty of Englishmen regard all French dishes as 'concoctions.'"

"H'm," said her husband. "All the same, it's a piece of damned impertinence for him to criticize our cook to you."

"He really didn't mean it that way, Donald. Though, as a matter of fact, I don't think things have been quite up to her usual standard lately. I must look into it."

Dr. Solway shook his head.

"I can't see any need for that. Her meals always seem perfectly good to me."

"All the same, I think just a word wouldn't come amiss."

"Better not to risk upsetting her. Cooks of any kind are pretty hard to come by nowadays," he suggested.

"Harder than assistants are? No, this, at least, is my department, Donald."

"Yes, of course, my dear. It's only that cooks are so touchy. . . ."

• • •

Curiously, it was quite some little time later—a week or so, in fact, after Helen had discovered herself to be pregnant again—that an appalling thought struck her. It came from nowhere and impinged with a vivid clarity on her half-awake mind in the small hours of one morning. A revelation-type thought: Once it had struck, she knew with a positive conviction that it was right. It caused her to lift herself on one elbow, switch on the light and thump her sleeping husband hard on the back, so that he started up, dazzled and bewildered.

"You cad!" she told him. "You dirty cheat! It's the meanest, most despicable trick I ever heard of. I'll— I'll——"

Words deserted her while her husband screwed up his eyes at her. His own temper had risen.

"How dare you do that!" he exclaimed. "It's a most dangerous thing to startle a sleeping man like——"

"How dare *I*! That's good. I suppose you're going to deny it."

"Deny what?" he inquired.

"Yes, I thought you would. Well, let me tell you it's no good. I know when you're lying, Donald."

He peered at her more closely.

"For heaven's sake! What on earth is all this about?"

"You know very well."

"But I——"

"Oh, yes, you do. No wonder cook gave notice. It was *you* all the time. *You* were doing something to the food—'treating' it, as you called it. And of all the low-down, repulsive, rotten, sly things to do! You knew just what I thought about your idea, and you deliberately sneaked in and did it behind my back, *and* left cook to carry the blame."

"I never blamed anyone. I said——"

"Don't you try to justify it. I'm not listening. How

dare you do your beastly experiments on me! Oh, I was never so humiliated!"

Dr. Solway gave it up and ceased to dissemble.

"All right, then. I did. But it wasn't just on you, it was on *us*—me, too. And to call it a 'beastly experiment' is simply emotional nonsense. It is immensely important: The outcome of it may enable the whole human race to take a great leap forward."

"What do I care whether it leaps? I'm interested in me and my baby. You knew perfectly well what my feelings were, and you didn't care a damn. You just cold-bloodedly cheated. . . . All right, if that's all you care about me, we've come to the end. . . . I shall leave you. . . . I shall get a divorce. . . . I shall——"

"Ah!" said her husband.

She checked, suddenly.

"What do you mean, 'Ah!' like that?" she demanded.

"I was thinking of the publicity. It will be bound to arouse great interest in the results."

She glared at him.

"Well, then, I probably shan't get a divorce. Though if treating one's wife like a laboratory animal isn't good grounds for divorce, there must be something very wrong with the law. . . .

"But I shall go. I shall certainly go—and take the children with me. Who knows what you might do with them after this. I shall go this very morning. I can't bear to be in the same house with you another day. . . ."

But, somehow, with the coming of daylight and the familiar routine, the need to shake off the dust did not seem quite so urgent. There were the difficulties of knowing *where* to go, and what to do about the children's schools, and getting things packed, and not having enough ready cash available, and one thing and another that caused her to decide that next week would have to do. So she only got as far as moving herself into the spare bedroom for the few days it would take to make the arrangements. Then what had looked like a simple, decisive action seemed to sprout complications. The matter of the coming baby presented an additional problem, making the whole thing seem too much to cope with just then, and she decided she would have to postpone it till that was over. So presently she moved herself back into the best bedroom and banished Donald to the spare room, making it quite clear that she had no intention of forgiving him, and keeping him aware of it.

"It's the underhandedness, the disloyalty of it more than anything," she complained. "How can I ever trust you again after an unforgivable thing like that? And what sort of a marriage is it when people don't trust each other? You've simply broken up our life together by trying to cheat me into furthering your own career. It was a low, nasty thing to even think of doing, and I pray every night that you'll be disappointed in the end. If there's any justice, you will. . . ."

• • •

In due course, the baby arrived.

When Helen Solway had left for the nursing home, her misgivings—though she determinedly disguised them from her husband under a confident nonchalance —had been considerable. When he visited her there, her anxieties had already been relaxed, and when she returned home, it was in a mood of triumphant satisfaction. She lost no time at all in dimming any hopes he might still have.

"And so," she concluded, "all your silly scheming was simply wasted after all. You made all that unpleasantness for nothing. It serves you right. He's a lovely baby. I had the doctor there give him a specially careful examination, and he says he's a very fine baby, and *perfectly* normal in every way."

Dr. Solway looked down at the baby as she held it. He opened his mouth to reply, thought better of it and contented himself with inspecting the small countenance closely. It looked, he found, quite disappointingly like almost any other baby.

The household settled down again, and the new baby took its place in it.

Doctor Solway's hopes had undoubtedly flickered low, but he would not let them die. He adopted a habit of visiting the baby several times a day for the purpose of studying it lengthily and intently.

After a fortnight or so of this, his wife forbade the practice on the grounds that it disturbed the baby and made it nervous.

"It frightens him so that he gets restless," she declared. "Just think how you'd feel if you were his size and had to look up at a great solemn face staring down at you for hours a day. It isn't fair on him."

So Dr. Solway saw less of the baby. And by degrees it somehow came about that he was scarcely seeing anything of it at all. One day it occurred to him that his wife was looking a little peaky, and that led him on to notice that she was unusually quiet and a little distrait in manner. A slight suspicion began to take a firmer hold. He made a forthright approach:

"Just why are you keeping the baby hidden away so much now?" he inquired, covering his sudden hope with artificial calmness of manner.

"Hidden away!" she repeated. "Why, Donald, what nonsense! It's just that he's better when he's quiet. He so easily gets upset. I think he must be very sensitive."

Her husband regarded her for a moment.

"That doesn't sound very convincing, my dear."

"Well, really! I don't think I quite understand you, Donald."

"No? Then I'd better explain, hadn't I? I rather think you don't want me to see the baby—not for more than a moment at a time. Now why could that be? Could it, perhaps, be because you don't want me to perceive certain signs that our experiment was not entirely unsuccessful after all? Could it be that?"

"Of course not, Donald. What rubbish! I told you the doctor said he was a perfectly normal——"

"Ah, yes. But that *was* several weeks ago, my dear. Come to think of it, one was perhaps a little too eager. An unusual ability could not very well be perceptible until some means to express it had developed, could it?"

"You're talking silly nonsense, Donald. He's just a nice, perfectly normal, happy little baby."

"I thought you said he was sensitive and easily upset?"

"Well, I mean he could easily be upset. It's better not to disturb him."

"All the same, I think I'll go up and just take a look at him."

"I'd rather you didn't, Donald. He's probably just gone to sleep."

"You *are* anxious to keep me away from him. I'm sorry, my dear. It's no good standing in my way like that. I intend to see what this is all about. You come, too, by all means, if you wish to."

He went past her into the hall and started up the stairs. Helen stood for a moment clenching her hands, working them wretchedly together; then she turned and followed him with a dragging step.

Dr. Solway's imposed calmness was breaking down. Excitement surged up in him as he approached the door of the baby's nursery. Helen's reluctance had been so transparent that she might almost as well have confirmed his deductions in words. He no longer had any doubt that the experiment had not completely failed, but the extent of its success—whether it would be decisive enough to let him face his critics with his own son as living evidence in support of his theories—that was what he was about to find out. . . .

His hand shook as he reached for the knob and let himself into the room.

The baby was not asleep. He was lying on his back, blue eyes very wide open, making quiet baby noises. He became aware of them as they approached the cot and stood beside it. The blue eyes focused, and he smiled up at Dr. Solway. Then he rolled his head on his pillow so that he was looking at his mother. The smile widened and then disappeared. The little lips opened and shut.

Dr. Solway was tense with excitement. He was convinced in that moment that the baby was trying to speak.

He bent closer, determined to catch anything that might sound even remotely like an attempt at a word. Helen Solway stood with her hands still clasped tightly together, an imploring look on her face.

"Ma——" said the baby, but got no further.

The tiny lips opened and shut again, as if, it seemed to Dr. Solway, working up for another try. Then the mouth pursed. The baby's blue eyes looked up yearningly at his mother. Then the lips opened once more. The articulation was not sharp, for lack of teeth, but he spoke; the words were quite clear:

"*Maman,*" said the baby, "*j'ai faim.*"

So Pete Crocker, the sheriff of Barnstable County, which was the whole of Cape Cod, came into the Federal Ethical Suicide Parlor in Hyannis one May afternoon—and he told the two six-foot Hostesses there that they weren't to be alarmed, but that a notorious nothinghead named Billy the Poet was believed headed for the Cape.

A nothinghead was a person who refused to take his ethical birth-control pills three times a day. The penalty for that was $10,000 and ten years in jail.

This was at a time when the population of Earth was 17 billion human beings. That was far too many mammals that big for a planet that small. The people were virtually packed together like drupelets.

Drupelets are the pulpy little knobs that compose the outside of a raspberry.

So the World Government was making a two-pronged attack on overpopulation. One pronging was the encouragement of ethical suicide, which consisted of going to the nearest Suicide Parlor and asking a

Hostess to kill you painlessly while you lay on a Barca-lounger. The other pronging was compulsory ethical birth control.

The sheriff told the Hostesses, who were pretty, tough-minded, highly intelligent girls, that roadblocks were being set up and house-to-house searches were being conducted to catch Billy the Poet. The main difficulty was that the police didn't know what he looked like. The few people who had seen him and known him for what he was were women—and they disagreed fantastically as to his height, his hair color, his voice, his weight, the color of his skin.

"I don't need to remind you girls," the sheriff went on, "that a nothinghead is very sensitive from the waist down. If Billy the Poet somehow slips in here and starts making trouble, one good kick in the right place will do wonders."

He was referring to the fact that ethical birth-control pills, the only legal form of birth control, made people numb from the waist down.

Most men said their bottom halves felt like cold iron or balsa wood. Most women said their bottom halves felt like wet cotton or stale ginger ale. The pills were so effective that you could blindfold a man who had taken one, tell him to recite the Gettysburg Address, kick him in the balls while he was doing it, and he wouldn't miss a syllable.

The pills were ethical because they didn't interfere with a person's ability to reproduce, which would have been unnatural and immoral. All the pills did was take every bit of pleasure out of sex.

Thus did science and morals go hand in hand.

• • •

The two Hostesses there in Hyannis were Nancy McLuhan and Mary Kraft. Nancy was a strawberry blonde. Mary was a glossy brunette. Their uniforms were white lipstick, heavy eye make-up, purple body stockings with nothing underneath and black leather boots. They ran a small operation—with only six suicide booths. In a really good week, say the one before Christmas, they might put 60 people to sleep. It was done with a hypodermic syringe.

"My main message to you two girls," said Sheriff Crocker, "is that everything's well under control. You can just go about your business here."

"Didn't you leave out part of your main message?" Nancy asked him.

"I don't get you."

"I didn't hear you say he was probably headed straight for us."

He shrugged in clumsy innocence. "We don't know that for sure."

"I thought that was all anybody *did* know about Billy the Poet: that he specializes in deflowering Hostesses in Ethical Suicide Parlors." Nancy was a virgin. All Hostesses were virgins. They also had to hold advanced degrees in psychology and nursing. They also had to be plump and rosy, and at least six feet tall.

America had changed in many ways, but it had yet to adopt the metric system.

Nancy McLuhan was burned up that the sheriff would try to protect her and Mary from the full truth about Billy the Poet—as though they might panic if they heard it. She told the sheriff so.

"How long do you think a girl would last in the E. S. S.," she said, meaning the Ethical Suicide Service, "if she scared *that* easy?"

The sheriff took a step backward, pulled in his chin. "Not very long, I guess."

"That's very true," said Nancy, closing the distance

between them and offering him a sniff of the edge of her hand, which was poised for a karate chop. All Hostesses were experts at judo and karate. "If you'd like to find out how helpless we are, just come toward me pretending you're Billy the Poet."

The sheriff shook his head, gave her a glassy smile. "I'd rather not."

"That's the smartest thing you've said today," said Nancy, turning her back on him while Mary laughed. "We're not scared—we're *angry*. Or we're not even *that*. He isn't *worth* that. We're *bored*. How boring that he should come a great distance, should cause all this fuss, in order to——" She let the sentence die there. "It's just too absurd."

"I'm not as mad at *him* as I am at the women who let him do it to them without a struggle," said Mary, "who let him do it and then couldn't tell the police what he looked like. Suicide Hostesses at that!"

"Somebody hasn't been keeping up with her karate," said Nancy.

• • •

It wasn't just Billy the Poet who was attracted to Hostesses in Ethical Suicide Parlors. All nothingheads were. Bombed out of their skulls with the sex madness that came from taking nothing, they thought the white lips and big eyes and body stocking and boots of a Hostess spelled *sex, sex, sex*.

The truth was, of course, that sex was the last thing any Hostess ever had in mind.

"If Billy follows his usual M. O.," said the sheriff, "he'll study your habits and the neighborhood. And then he'll pick one or the other of you and he'll send her a dirty poem in the mail."

"Charming," said Nancy.

"He has also been known to use the telephone."

"How brave," said Nancy. Over the sheriff's shoulder, she could see the mailman coming.

A blue light went on over the door of a booth. The person in there wanted something. It was the only booth in use at the time.

The sheriff asked her if there was a possibility that the person in there was Billy the Poet, and Nancy said, "Well, if it is, I can break his neck with my thumb and forefinger."

"Foxy Grandpa," said Mary, who'd seen him, too. A Foxy Grandpa was any old man, cute and senile, who quibbled and joked and reminisced for hours before he let a hostess put him to sleep.

Nancy rolled her eyes. "We've spent the past two hours trying to decide on a last meal."

And then the mailman came in with just one letter. It was addressed to Nancy in smeary pencil. She was splendid with anger and disgust as she opened it, knowing it would be a piece of filth from Billy.

She was right. Inside the envelope was a poem. It wasn't an original poem. It was a song from olden days that had taken on new meanings since the numbness of ethical birth control had become universal. It went like this, in smeary pencil again:

> We were walking through the park,
> A-goosing statues in the dark.
> If Sherman's horse can take it,
> So can you.

When Nancy came into the suicide booth to see what he wanted, the Foxy Grandpa was lying on the mint-green Barcalounger where hundreds had died so peacefully over the years. He was studying the menu from the Howard Johnson's next door and beating time to the Muzak coming from the loud-speaker on the lemon-yellow wall. The room was painted cinder block. There was one barred window with a Venetian blind.

There was a Howard Johnson's next door to every Ethical Suicide Parlor, and vice versa. The Howard Johnson's had an orange roof and the Suicide Parlor had a purple roof, but they were both the Government. Practically everything was the Government.

Practically everything was automated, too. Nancy and Mary and the sheriff were lucky to have jobs. Most people didn't. The average citizen moped around home and watched television, which was the Government. Every 15 minutes his television would urge him to vote intelligently or consume intelligently, or worship in the church of his choice, or love his fellow men, or obey the laws—or pay a call to the nearest Ethical Suicide Parlor and find out how friendly and understanding a Hostess could be.

The Foxy Grandpa was something of a rarity since he was marked by old age, was bald, was shaky, had spots on his hands. Most people looked 22, thanks to antiaging shots they took twice a year. That the old man looked old was proof that the shots had been discovered after his sweet bird of youth had flown.

"Have we decided on a last supper yet?" Nancy asked him. She heard peevishness in her own voice, heard herself betray her exasperation with Billy the Poet, her boredom with the old man. She was ashamed, for this was unprofessional of her. "The breaded veal cutlet is very good."

The old man cocked his head. With the greedy cunning of second childhood, he had caught her being unprofessional, unkind, and he was going to punish her for it. "You don't sound very friendly. I thought you were all supposed to be friendly. I thought this was supposed to be a pleasant place to come."

"I beg your pardon," she said. "If I seem unfriendly, it has nothing to do with you."

"I thought maybe I bored you."

"No, no," she said gamely, "not at all. You certainly know some very interesting history." Among other things, the Foxy Grandpa claimed to have known J. Edgar Nation, the Grand Rapids druggist who was the father of ethical birth control.

"Then *look* like you're interested," he told her. He could get away with that sort of impudence. The thing was, he could leave any time he wanted to, right up to the moment he asked for the needle—and he had to *ask* for the needle. That was the law.

Nancy's art, and the art of every Hostess, was to see that volunteers didn't leave, to coax and wheedle and flatter them patiently every step of the way.

So Nancy had to sit down there in the booth, to pretend to marvel at the yarn the old man told, a story everybody knew, about how J. Edgar Nation happened to experiment with ethical birth control.

"He didn't have the slightest idea his pills would be taken by human beings someday," said the Foxy Grandpa. "His dream was to introduce morality into the monkey house at the Grand Rapids Zoo. Did you realize that?" he inquired severely.

"No. No, I didn't. That's very interesting."

"He and his eleven kids went to church one Easter. And the day was so nice and the Easter service had been so beautiful and pure that they decided to take a walk through the zoo, and they were just walking on clouds."

"Um." The scene described was lifted from a play that was performed on television every Easter.

The Foxy Grandpa shoehorned himself into the

scene, had himself chat with the Nations just before they got to the monkey house. " 'Good morning, Mr. Nation,' I said to him. 'It certainly is a nice morning.' 'And a good morning to *you*, Mr. Howard,' he said to me. 'There is nothing like an Easter morning to make a man feel clean and reborn and at one with God's intentions.' "

"Um." Nancy could hear the telephone ringing faintly, naggingly, through the nearly soundproof door.

"So we went on to the monkey house together, and what do you think we saw?"

"I can't imagine." Somebody answered the phone.

"We saw a monkey playing with his private parts!"

"No!"

"Yes! And J. Edgar Nation was so upset he went straight home and he started developing a pill that would make monkeys in the springtime fit things for a Christian family to see."

There was a knock on the door.

"Yes?" said Nancy.

"Nancy," said Mary, "telephone for you."

When Nancy came out of the booth, she found the sheriff choking on little squeals of law-enforcement delight. The telephone was tapped by agents hidden in the Howard Johnson's. Billy the Poet was believed to be on the line. His call had been traced. Police were already on their way to grab him.

"Keep him on, keep him on," the sheriff whispered to Nancy, and he gave her the telephone as though it were solid gold.

"Yes?" said Nancy.

"Nancy McLuhan?" said a man. His voice was disguised. He might have been speaking through a kazoo. "I'm calling for a mutual friend."

"Oh?"

"He asked me to deliver a message."

"I see."

"It's a poem."

"All right."

"Ready?"

"Ready." Nancy could hear sirens screaming in the background of the call.

The caller must have heard the sirens, too, but he recited the poem without emotion. It went like this:

"Soak yourself in Jergen's Lotion.
Here comes the one-man population explosion."

They got him. Nancy heard it all—the thumping and clumping, the argle-bargle and cries.

The depression she felt as she hung up was glandular. Her brave body had prepared for a fight that was not to be.

The sheriff bounded out of the Suicide Parlor in such a hurry to see the famous criminal he'd helped catch that a sheaf of papers fell from the pocket of his trench coat.

Mary picked them up, called after the sheriff. He halted for a moment, said the papers didn't matter anymore, asked her if maybe she wouldn't like to come along. There was a flurry between the two girls, with Nancy persuading Mary to go, declaring that she had no curiosity about Billy. So Mary left, irrelevantly handing the sheaf to Nancy.

The sheaf proved to be photocopies of poems Billy had sent to Hostesses in other places. Nancy read the top one. It made much of a peculiar side effect of ethical birth-control pills: They not only made people numb—they also made people piss blue. The poem was called *What the Somethinghead Said to the Suicide Hostess,* and it went like this:

> *I did not sow, I did not spin,*
> *And thanks to pills, I did not sin.*
> *I loved the crowds, the stink, the*
>   *noise.*
> *And when I peed, I peed turquoise.*
>
> *I ate beneath a roof of orange;*
> *Swung with progress like a door*
>   *hinge.*
> *'Neath purple roof I've come today*
> *To piss my azure life away.*
>
> *Virgin Hostess, death's recruiter,*
> *Life is cute, but you are cuter.*
> *Mourn my pecker, purple daughter—*
> *All it passed was sky-blue water.*

"You never heard that story before—about how J. Edgar Nation came to invent ethical birth control?" the Foxy Grandpa wanted to know. His voice cracked.

"Never did," lied Nancy.

"I thought everybody knew that."

"It was news to me."

"When he got through with the monkey house, you couldn't tell it from the Michigan Supreme Court. Meanwhile, there was this crisis going on in the United Nations. The people who understood science said people had to quit reproducing so much, and the people who understood morals said society would collapse if people used sex for nothing but pleasure."

The Foxy Grandpa got off his Barcalounger, went over to the window, pried two slats of the blind apart. There wasn't much to see out there. The view was blocked by the backside of a mocked-up thermometer 20 feet high, which faced the street. It was calibrated in billions of people on Earth, from 0 to 20. The make-believe column of liquid was a strip of translucent red plastic. It showed how many people there were on Earth. Very close to the bottom was a black arrow showing what the population ought to be.

The Foxy Grandpa was looking at the setting sun through that red plastic, and through the blind, too, so that his face was banded with shadows and red.

"Tell me," he said, "when I die, how much will that thermometer go down? A foot?"

"No."

"An inch?"

"Not quite."

"You know what the answer is, don't you?" he said, and he faced her. The senility had vanished from his voice and eyes. "One inch on that thing equals 83,333,333 people. You knew that, didn't you?"

"That—that might be true," said Nancy, "but that isn't the right way to look at it, in my opinion."

He didn't ask her what the right way was, in her opinion. He completed a thought of his own, instead. "I'll tell you something else that's true: I'm Billy the Poet, and you're a very good-looking woman."

With one hand, he drew a snub-nosed revolver from his belt. With the other, he peeled off his bald dome and wrinkled forehead, which proved to be rubber. Now he looked 22.

"The police will want to know exactly what I look like when this is all over," he told Nancy with a malicious grin. "In case you're not good at describing people, and it's surprising how many women aren't:

> *I'm five foot two,*
> *With eyes of blue,*
> *With brown hair to my shoulders—*
> *A manly elf*
> *So full of self*
> *The ladies say he smolders."*

Billy was ten inches shorter than Nancy was. She had about 40 pounds on him. She told him he didn't have a chance, but Nancy was much mistaken. He had unbolted the bars on the window the night before and he made her go out the window and then down a manhole that was hidden from the street by the big thermometer.

He took her down into the sewers of Hyannis. He knew where he was going. He had a flashlight and a map. Nancy had to go before him along the narrow catwalk, her own shadow dancing mockingly in the lead. She tried to guess where they were, relative to the real world above. She guessed correctly when they passed under the Howard Johnson's, guessed from noises she heard. The machinery that processed and served the food there was silent. But, so people wouldn't feel too lonesome when eating there, the designers had provided sound effects for the kitchen. It was these Nancy heard—a tape recording of the clashing of silverware and the laughter of Negroes and Puerto Ricans.

After that she was lost. Billy had very little to say to her other than "Right," or "Left," or "Don't try anything funny, Juno, or I'll blow your great big fucking head off."

Only once did they have anything resembling a conversation, Billy began it, and ended it, too. "What in hell is a girl with hips like yours doing selling death?" he asked her from behind.

She dared to stop. "I can answer that," she told him. She was confident that she could give him an answer that would shrivel him like napalm.

But he gave her a shove, and offered to blow her head off again.

"You don't even want to hear my answer," she

taunted him. "You're afraid to hear it."

"I never listen to a woman till the pills wear off," sneered Billy. That was his plan, then—to keep her a prisoner for at least eight hours. That was how long it took for the pills to wear off.

"That's a silly rule."

"A woman's not a woman till the pills wear off."

"You certainly manage to make a woman feel like an object rather than a person."

"Thank the pills for that," said Billy.

• • •

There were 80 miles of sewers under Greater Hyannis, which had a population of 400,000 drupelets, 400,000 souls. Nancy lost track of the time down there. When Billy announced that they had at last reached their destination, it was possible for Nancy to imagine that a year had passed.

She tested this spooky impression by pinching her own thigh, by feeling what the chemical clock of her body said. Her thigh was still numb.

Billy ordered her to climb iron rungs that were set in wet masonry. There was a circle of sickly light above. It proved to be moonlight filtered through the plastic polygons of an enormous geodesic dome. Nancy didn't have to ask the traditional victim's question, "Where am I?" There was only one dome like that on Cape Cod. It was in Hyannis Port and it sheltered the ancient Kennedy Compound.

It was a museum of how life had been lived in more expansive times. The museum was closed. It was open only in the summertime.

The manhole from which Nancy and then Billy emerged was set in an expanse of green cement, which showed where the Kennedy lawn had been. On the green cement, in front of the ancient frame houses, were statues representing the 14 Kennedys who had been Presidents of the United States or the World. They were playing touch football.

The President of the World at the time of Nancy's abduction, incidentally, was an ex-Suicide Hostess named "Ma" Kennedy. Her statue would never join this particular touch-football game. Her name was Kennedy, all right, but she wasn't the real thing. People complained of her lack of style, found her vulgar. On the wall of her office was a sign that said, YOU DON'T HAVE TO BE CRAZY TO WORK HERE, BUT IT SURE HELPS, and another one that said, THIMK!, and another one that said, SOMEDAY WE'RE GOING TO HAVE TO GET ORGANIZED AROUND HERE.

Her office was in the Taj Mahal.

• • •

Until she arrived in the Kennedy Museum, Nancy McLuhan was confident that she would sooner or later get a chance to break every bone in Billy's little body, maybe even shoot him with his own gun. She wouldn't have minded doing those things. She thought he was more disgusting than a blood-filled tick.

It wasn't compassion that changed her mind. It was the discovery that Billy had a gang. There were at least eight people around the manhole, men and women in equal numbers, with stockings pulled over their heads. It was the women who laid firm hands on Nancy, told her to keep calm. They were all at least as tall as Nancy and they held her in places where they could hurt her like hell if they had to.

Nancy closed her eyes, but this didn't protect her from the obvious conclusion: These perverted women were sisters from the Ethical Suicide Service. This upset her so much that she asked loudly and bitterly, "How can you violate your oaths like this?"

She was promptly hurt so badly that she doubled up and burst into tears.

When she straightened up again, there was plenty more she wanted to say, but she kept her mouth shut. She speculated silently as to what on earth could make Suicide Hostesses turn against every concept of human decency. Nothingheadedness alone couldn't begin to explain it. They had to be drugged besides.

Nancy went over in her mind all the terrible drugs she'd learned about in school, persuaded herself that the women had taken the worst one of all. That drug was so powerful, Nancy's teachers had told her, that even a person numb from the waist down would copulate repeatedly and enthusiastically after just one glass. That had to be the answer: The women, and probably the men, too, had been drinking gin.

• • •

They hastened Nancy into the middle frame house which was dark like all the rest, and Nancy heard the men giving Billy the news. It was in this news that Nancy perceived a glint of hope. Help might be on its way.

The gang member who had phoned Nancy obscenely had fooled the police into believing that they had captured Billy the Poet, which was bad for Nancy. The police didn't know yet that Nancy was missing, two men told Billy, and a telegram had been sent to Mary Kraft in Nancy's name, declaring that Nancy had been called to New York City on urgent family business.

That was where Nancy saw the glint of hope: Mary wouldn't believe that telegram. Mary knew Nancy had no family in New York. Not one of the 63,000,000 people living there was a relative of Nancy's.

The gang had deactivated the burglar-alarm system

of the museum. They had also cut through a lot of the chains and ropes that were meant to keep visitors from touching anything of value. There was no mystery as to who and what had done the cutting. One of the men was armed with brutal lopping shears.

They marched Nancy into a servant's bedroom upstairs. The man with the shears cut the ropes that fenced off the narrow bed. They put Nancy into the bed and two men held Nancy while a woman gave her a knockout shot.

Billy the Poet had disappeared.

As Nancy was going under, the woman who had given her the shot asked her how old she was.

Nancy was determined not to answer, but discovered that the drug had made her powerless not to answer. "Sixty-three," she murmured.

"How does it feel to be a virgin at sixty-three?"

Nancy heard her own answer through a velvet fog. She was amazed by the answer, wanted to protest that it couldn't possibly be hers. "Pointless," she'd said.

Moments later, she asked the woman thickly, "What was in that needle?"

"What was in the needle, honey bunch? Why, honey bunch, they call that 'truth serum.'"

• • •

The moon was down when Nancy woke up—but the night was still out there. The shades were drawn and there was candlelight. Nancy had never seen a lit candle before.

What awakened Nancy was a dream of mosquitoes and bees. Mosquitoes and bees were extinct. So were birds. But Nancy dreamed that millions of insects swarmed about her from the waist down. They didn't sting. They fanned her. She was a nothinghead.

She went to sleep again. When she awoke next

time, she was being led into a bathroom by three
women, still with stockings over their heads. The bathroom was already filled with the steam from somebody
else's bath. There were somebody else's wet footprints
crisscrossing the floor and the air reeked of pine-needle
perfume.

Her will and intelligence returned as she was bathed
and perfumed and dressed in a white nightgown.
When the women stepped back to admire her, she
said to them quietly, "I may be a nothinghead now.
But that doesn't mean I have to think like one or act
like one."

Nobody argued with her.

• • •

Nancy was taken downstairs and out of the house.
She fully expected to be sent down a manhole again.
It would be the perfect setting for her violation by
Billy, she was thinking—down in a sewer.

But they took her across the green cement, where
the grass used to be, and then across the yellow cement,
where the beach used to be, and then out onto the
blue cement, where the harbor used to be. There were
26 yachts that had belonged to various Kennedys sunk
up to their water lines in blue cement. It was to the
most ancient of these yachts, the Marlin, once the
property of Joseph P. Kennedy, that they delivered
Nancy.

It was dawn. Because of the high-rise apartments all
around the Kennedy Museum, it would be an hour
before any direct sunlight would reach the microcosm
under the geodesic dome.

Nancy was escorted as far as the companionway to
the forward cabin of the Marlin. The women pan-
tomimed that she was expected to go down the five
steps alone.

Nancy froze for the moment and so did the women. And there were two actual statues in the tableau on the bridge. Standing at the wheel was a statue of Frank Wirtanen, once skipper of the Marlin. And next to him was his son and first mate, Carly. They weren't paying any attention to poor Nancy. They were staring out through the windshield at the blue cement.

Nancy, barefoot and wearing a thin white nightgown, descended bravely into the forward cabin, which was a pool of candlelight and pine-needle perfume. The companionway hatch was closed and locked behind her.

Nancy's emotions and the antique furnishings of the cabin were so complex that Nancy could not at first separate Billy the Poet from his surroundings, from all the mahogany and leaded glass. And then she saw him at the far end of the cabin, with his back against the door to the forward cockpit. He was wearing purple silk pajamas with a Russian collar. They were piped in red, and writhing across Billy's silken breast was a golden dragon. It was belching fire.

Anticlimactically, Billy was wearing glasses. He was holding a book.

Nancy poised herself on the next-to-the-bottom step, took a firm grip on the handholds in the companionway. She bared her teeth, calculated that it would take ten men Billy's size to dislodge her.

Between them was a great table. Nancy had expected the cabin to be dominated by a bed, possibly in the shape of a swan, but the Marlin was a day boat. The cabin was anything but a seraglio. It was about as voluptuous as a lower-middle-class dining room in Akron, Ohio, around 1910.

A candle was on the table. So were an ice bucket

and two glasses and a quart of champagne. Champagne was as illegal as heroin.

Billy took off his glasses, gave her a shy, embarrassed smile, said "Welcome."

"This is as far as I come."

He accepted that. "You're very beautiful there."

"And what am I supposed to say—that you're stunningly handsome? That I feel an overwhelming desire to throw myself into your manly arms?"

"If you wanted to make me happy, that would certainly be the way to do it." He said that humbly.

"And what about *my* happiness?"

The question seemed to puzzle him. "Nancy—that's what this is all about."

"What if my idea of happiness doesn't coincide with yours?"

"And what do you think my idea of happiness is?"

"I'm not going to throw myself into your arms, and I'm not going to drink that poison, and I'm not going to budge from here unless somebody makes me," said Nancy. "So I think your idea of happiness is going to turn out to be eight people holding me down on that table, while you bravely hold a cocked pistol to my head—and do what you want. That's the way it's going to have to be, so call your friends and get it over with!"

Which he did.

•   •   •

He didn't hurt her. He deflowered her with a clinical skill she found ghastly. When it was all over, he didn't seem cocky or proud. On the contrary, he was terribly depressed, and he said to Nancy, "Believe me, if there'd been any other way——"

Her reply to this was a face like stone—and silent tears of humiliation.

His helpers let down a folding bunk from the wall. It was scarcely wider than a bookshelf and hung on chains. Nancy allowed herself to be put to bed in it, and she was left alone with Billy the Poet again. Big as she was, like a double bass wedged onto that narrow shelf, she felt like a pitiful little thing. A scratchy, war-surplus blanket had been tucked in around her. It was her own idea to pull up a corner of the blanket to hide her face.

Nancy sensed from sounds what Billy was doing, which wasn't much. He was sitting at the table, sighing occasionally, sniffing occasionally, turning the pages of a book. He lit a cigar and the stink of it seeped under her blanket. Billy inhaled the cigar, then coughed and coughed and coughed.

When the coughing died down, Nancy said loathingly through the blanket, "You're so strong, so masterful, so healthy. How wonderful to be so manly."

Billy only sighed at this.

"I'm not a very typical nothinghead," she said. "I hated it—hated everything about it."

Billy sniffed, turned a page.

"I suppose all the other women just loved it—couldn't get enough of it."

"Nope."

She uncovered her face. "What do you mean, 'Nope'?"

"They've all been like you."

This was enough to make Nancy sit up and stare at him. "The women who helped you tonight——"

"What about them?"

"You've done to them what you did to me?"

He didn't look up from his book. "That's right."

"Why don't they kill you instead of helping you?"

"Because they understand." And then he added mildly, "They're *grateful*."

Nancy got out of bed, came to the table, gripped the edge of the table, leaned close to him. And she said to him tautly, "I am not grateful."

"You will be."

"And what could possibly bring about that miracle?"

"Time," said Billy.

Billy closed his book, stood up. Nancy was confused by his magnetism. Somehow he was very much in charge again.

"What you've been through, Nancy," he said, "is a typical wedding night for a strait-laced girl of a hundred years ago, when everybody was a nothing-head. The groom did without helpers because the bride wasn't customarily ready to kill him. Otherwise, the spirit of the occasion was much the same. These are the pajamas my great-great-grandfather wore on his wedding night in Niagara Falls.

"According to his diary, his bride cried all that night and threw up twice. But, with the passage of time, she became a sexual enthusiast."

It was Nancy's turn to reply by not replying. She understood the tale. It frightened her to understand so easily that, from gruesome beginnings, sexual enthusiasm could grow and grow.

"You're a very typical nothinghead," said Billy. "If you dare to think about it now, you'll realize that you're angry because I'm such a bad lover, and a funny-looking shrimp besides. And what you can't help dreaming about from now on is a really suitable mate for a Juno like yourself.

"You'll find him, too—tall and strong and gentle. The nothinghead movement is growing by leaps and bounds."

"But——" said Nancy, and she stopped there. She looked out a porthole at the rising sun.

"But what?"

"The world is in the mess it is today because of the nothingheadedness of olden times. Don't you see?" She was pleading weakly. "The world can't afford sex anymore."

"Of course it can afford sex," said Billy. "All it can't afford anymore is reproduction."

"Then why the laws?"

"They're bad laws," said Billy. "If you go back through history, you'll find that the people who have been most eager to rule, to make the laws, to enforce the laws and to tell everybody exactly how God Almighty wants things here on earth—those people have forgiven themselves and their friends for anything and everything. But they have been absolutely disgusted and terrified by the natural sexuality of common men and women.

"Why this is, I do not know. That is one of the many questions I wish somebody would ask the machines. I do know this: The triumph of that sort of disgust and terror is now complete. Almost every man and woman looks and feels like something the cat dragged in. The only sexual beauty that an ordinary human being can see today is in the woman who will kill him. Sex is death. There's a short and nasty equation for you: 'Sex is death. Q. E. D.'

"So you see, Nancy," said Billy, "I have spent this night, and many others like it, attempting to restore a certain amount of innocent pleasure to the world, which is poorer in pleasure than it needs to be."

Nancy sat down quietly and bowed her head.

"I'll tell you what my grandfather did on the dawn of his wedding night," said Billy.

"I don't think I want to hear it."

"It isn't violent. It's—it's meant to be tender."

"Maybe that's why I don't want to hear it."

"He read his bride a poem." Billy took the book from the table, opened it. "His diary tells which poem it was. While we aren't bride and groom, and while we may not meet again for years, I'd like to read this poem to you, to have you know I've loved you."

"Please—no. I couldn't stand it."

"All right. I'll leave the book here, with the place marked, in case you want to read it later. It's the poem beginning:

> 'How do I love thee? Let me count
>   the ways.
> I love thee to the depth and
>   breadth and height
> My soul can reach, when feeling
>   out of sight
> For the ends of Being and ideal
>   Grace.' "

Billy put a small bottle on top of the book. "I am also leaving you these pills. If you take one a month, you will never have children. And still you'll be a nothinghead."

And he left. And they all left but Nancy.

When Nancy raised her eyes at last to the book and bottle, she saw that there was a label on the bottle. What the label said was this:

WELCOME TO THE MONKEY HOUSE

Charles Shelton had been a desk clerk at the Hotel Madison for almost 30 years. He had watched it deteriorate from one of the finer hotels in the city to its present condition, just a shade better than a flophouse.

Shelton seldom thought about the good years. He was not one to live in the past. He lived from day to day, satisfied to sit behind the registration desk, reading his detective magazines and watching people come and go.

Sam Webster owned the Hotel Madison. He was over 60, had no hair, bulging eyes, and clothes that were almost as old and shabby as his building. He constantly worked a cigar around in his tight mouth, and when he was in the hotel he drank whiskey from a bottle he kept under Shelton's desk. Webster didn't believe in improvements. He had bought the Madison when it was almost new, and if he could find any excuse to avoid putting money into it, even if that meant chewing gum for the plumbing and Scotch tape for the cracked windows, he took it.

Sam came to the hotel about twice a week. He picked up the receipts from the safe behind the desk, nodded to Shelton and, occasionally, looked over the books. He was as tight with his conversation as he was with his money.

One Tuesday evening just after Shelton had come to work, Sam Webster came in, puffing on a damp cigar. His coat was wet from the cold drizzle outside and his glasses were covered with a gray mist. He nodded to Shelton, removed his coat and began to go over the books. When he had finished, he relighted his cigar, took four or five deep drags and said:

"Charlie, how long you been with me now?"

"Almost thirty years," Shelton said, looking up from his *True Detective* magazine.

"And so, after thirty years, you decide to start stealing from me? You don't think I pay you enough?"

"I don't understand, Mr. Webster."

"I don't understand, either. The books, they don't balance. The last few months, I noticed something's wrong. I figure either you are pocketing money or people aren't paying for their rooms. Which is it, Charlie?"

"Mr. Webster, I'm not a thief."

"You never seemed like one to me, but where is the money going? I'm asking you."

Sam Webster took a paper cup from the water cooler, the bottle of whiskey from beneath the desk, and poured himself a drink.

"Well, Charlie, I can have some auditors come in and figure out just how much is missing, or do you want to tell me about it?"

Shelton looked at the bottle of whiskey. He wished

that he had a drink. In 30 years, Sam Webster had never offered him anything.

Shelton cleared his throat. "It's a long story and a little involved, Mr. Webster. But to make it short—we don't always get paid."

"Charlie, as long as you been around, you know a hotel like this, they don't pay in advance, they gotta have luggage. Now, where is all the luggage for these people who skip out? You're not sleeping behind that desk, are you?"

Shelton wiped his forehead with his handkerchief. He took a drink of water from the cooler. His throat still felt dry. "It isn't that. It's Room 312. I noticed it about a year ago. I was going to tell you."

"What about 312? There's something wrong with the room? What is it? I don't want no repair bills."

"It's a little difficult to explain." Shelton was still perspiring. "It's like this, Mr. Webster, when someone checks into 312—they're gone. No one ever sees them again."

Sam Webster poured himself another drink and swallowed it in one gulp. "Charlie, I've known you for thirty years. Now, what the hell kind of story is that? Whata you mean—they're gone?"

"They're just gone, that's all. They disappear. If they check in after two A.M., they're all right, but if they take the room before that time, they're never here in the morning. Every trace is gone—luggage, everything. The way I figure it, it happens sometime between midnight and two A.M."

"Yeah, and just where do they go, Charlie?"

"I don't know, Mr. Webster. All the people I've checked into the room, I've never seen any of them again. That's why I usually keep it for the bums and the winos. Mostly, I just keep it empty."

"Charlie, you're sure you're not crazy? You're sure this really happens?"

"Mr. Webster, stay tonight. I'll check someone into Room 312."

Sam Webster picked up the telephone and called his wife.

"Honey," he said, "I won't be home tonight. A little trouble here at the hotel. No, nothing serious." He placed the receiver down on its cradle.

"Charlie, I stay in this dump all night and you feeding me a story, I ain't gonna like it."

"Mr. Webster, I've been with you almost thirty years."

"Yeah, I know. OK, I'm gonna have some dinner. Don't check anyone into 312 until I get back."

It was still raining when Sam Webster returned from dinner. Shelton had just finished a copy of *Official Detective* and was eating a sandwich he had had sent over from Rudy's Diner. Webster took off his wet coat and sat down in one of the overstuffed chairs in the lobby. He untied the laces of his shoes, loosened his tie and took a fresh cigar out of his pocket.

At eight o'clock, Shelton checked in a young couple from Waterloo, Iowa. At 8:30, two salesmen, and along toward nine o'clock, a seedy-looking bum in a tan overcoat. The bum had a wine bottle under his arm and Shelton got the three dollars in advance. He gave him the key to 312.

Sam Webster followed the tan overcoat into the elevator, got out with it on the third floor and watched it walk unsteadily into 312. He went down to the end of the hall, sat down in a wicker chair that was covered with dust and lighted another cigar. By 1:30 A.M. he had smoked eight cigars. At that hour, he got off the chair and took the elevator to the lobby.

Shelton was drinking coffee out of a green Thermos.

"Well," Sam Webster said, "almost two o'clock and nothing happened."

"There's nothing *to* happen," Shelton said. "At two o'clock, I'll take the passkey and we'll go up there and he'll be gone."

"Let's go now," Sam Webster said.

"It's almost two o'clock. I don't want to go into the room until I'm certain that it happened."

"I still can't believe it. I just can't believe it. This has gotta be some kind of crazy story."

At two A.M. sharp, Sam Webster grabbed the passkey and hurried into the elevator, with Shelton following him. Webster was breathing heavily when they got to 312. "You sure it's safe?" he asked. "I don't want to get hit by lightning or anything."

"There's no lightning," Shelton said.

Sam Webster opened the door a crack. The room was dark. He pushed the door all the way open. He waited for the clerk to precede him into the room. Shelton snapped the light on. The room was empty. The bed had been slept in, but there wasn't a trace of anyone or anything. No clothes, no wine bottle; everything was gone.

Webster looked around the room. He searched the bathroom and the closet. He looked under the bed twice.

"I can't believe it," he said. "I just can't believe it." He sat down on the bed and then jumped up, as though he were afraid he, too, might disappear. "Let's go," he said. Shelton locked the door and they took the elevator back to the lobby.

Sam Webster took the whiskey bottle from beneath the desk and poured two drinks. "Here's to us, Charlie," he said. "A toast."

"What are we toasting, Mr. Webster?"

Sam drank his whiskey. "I don't know. What the hell, this is really something big. There's bound to be some great thing we can do with this."

"Maybe we should call the police," Shelton said.

Sam Webster coughed whiskey all over himself. He was choking and his face was red. "Call the police! What the hell do we need the police for? We got a great discovery here. You call your wife and tell her you'll be late. We're going to work something out."

"I don't have to call my wife. I don't have a wife."

"No? What happened? I thought I met her a few years ago. A little woman with brown hair."

"That's right. She's not with me anymore. It'll be ten months the end of next week."

"Oh, I'm sorry to hear that, Charlie. How did it happen?"

"Well, to tell you the truth, it was Room 312. I got tired of her nagging. She was never satisfied with anything, not for the twenty years we were married. I arranged for her to stay in 312 one night."

Sam hit Shelton so hard on the back that he knocked the paper cup out of his hand.

"Charlie, that's it! You're a goddamn genius. I knew it all the time. You quiet types are always smart."

"I don't understand, Mr. Webster."

"Don't you see, Charlie, we get rid of people for a price. A damn good price. Our own little disposal service. No mess, no fuss. Do you know how *many* people there are that want to get rid of their wives, their mother-in-laws, business associates? All we have to do is spread the word in the right spots. We'll have more goddamn business for Room 312 than we can handle."

"Mr. Webster, isn't that just like murder?"

"Murder! Hell, no. Who said anything about murder? There's no bodies. Nobody can blame us for a thing. I'm gonna cut you in for twenty percent. Charlie, we'll both get rich."

"Twenty percent. That's very generous, Mr. Webster."

"Yeah, well, I'm a generous guy. There's only one thing I gotta do first—that's Hilda."

"Who's Hilda?"

"Hilda is Mrs. Webster. My goddamn miserable wife. Worst person ever walked the face of God's earth. She's got to go tomorrow night."

"So soon? Maybe you better think about it for a while, Mr. Webster."

"No chance! I wish it wasn't so late. I'd get her over here right now. Tomorrow night I'll get her in that room if I have to hit her over the head."

The next evening about ten, Sam Webster and Mrs. Webster walked into the Hotel Madison. As they passed the desk, he patted her arm and remarked that it was going to be like a second honeymoon. He had a cheap bottle of wine under his arm. He winked at Shelton as he led Hilda into the elevator. She was blushing like a schoolgirl.

Shortly after midnight, Sam Webster was in the lobby again.

"She's sleeping like a baby," he said. "Like a baby gorilla. That wine really did the trick. Two glasses and she was snoring so loud the room was shaking. Sounds just like a subway train. She even forgot about the honeymoon. Charlie, old baby, if this works, you get a bonus. An extra week's pay. I mean it. You don't know what it's been like living with that ape for the past thirty years."

"It'll work," Shelton said. "It always does."

At two A.M., Sam went up to 312. He was back in a few minutes, his face beaming. "It happened! Not a trace! Not a goddamn trace. Gone just like that," he snapped his fingers. "Even the wine bottle is gone. Can you imagine, Charlie, *no more Hilda.*" This time, he poured Shelton's drink first.

The next day, Sam Webster called an old friend of his, Louis Crowell. "Louie," he said, "Sammy Webster, yeah, I'm fine. How are you? And how's the Mrs.? I got a little business proposition for you, Louie. How about lunch and we'll talk it over?"

That night, Mr. and Mrs. Crowell checked in. Louis Crowell told his wife that Sam Webster wanted to sell the hotel, that he was almost giving it away. Louis wanted to stay in it a night or two to see if everything was OK.

In the lobby a little after midnight, Shelton handed Crowell the whiskey bottle and pointed to the paper cups. Louis poured himself a drink. "I don't like to see her get hurt too much," he said.

"Mr. Crowell, I can assure you there'll be no pain. Your wife will just conveniently disappear."

"That's what Sammy said. I don't want no trouble with the police."

"There'll be no trouble with anyone. At two o'clock, you can go back up to bed and get some sleep."

Early the next morning, Louis Crowell came down to Shelton's cubbyhole office at the rear of the desk and found Webster and the clerk waiting for him. Louis reached into his pocket and removed an envelope, which he handed to Sam Webster.

"You got a great thing going here, Sammy. You delivered just like you said you would."

Sam reached into the envelope and pulled out two $100 bills. "Here, Charlie, twenty percent, just like

I said." He turned to Louis Crowell. "Louie, you got a friend you think might like our service, give him my name."

"Sure, Sammy. I can send you lots of business. You'll be booked months in advance. You got the greatest thing since penicillin."

Sam Webster looked as if his horse had just won the Kentucky Derby. "It's more like the world's greatest wart remover," he said.

"You'll be a big man, Sammy," Louis said with obvious envy.

"Yeah," Sam Webster said with a faraway look in his eyes.

A month later, the demand was so heavy for Room 312 that the fee had gone up to $2000. Webster even had half a dozen suits made. He was slowly working his way through the chorus lines around town.

Shelton kept his money in the safe at the Madison. He had never once bothered to count it. One afternoon he did stop at a used-car lot, but when the salesman came toward him, he left hastily. He didn't know how to drive, anyway.

Walter Slater started the trouble. He had thin gray hair and eyes that always seemed close to tears. He came into the hotel one evening when Shelton had just come on duty. "Mr. Shelton," he said, "do you remember me?"

Shelton remembered the watery eyes. "Certainly I do, Mr. Slater. Almost a month ago, wasn't it?"

"Twenty-eight days," Walter Slater said.

"Don't tell me you want to rent 312 again? You'll be our first repeat customer."

"That isn't it, Mr. Shelton. You see, it's Martha, my wife."

"Yes, I remember her when you checked in," Shelton said nervously. "She has—uh—remained absent, hasn't she?"

"I want her back, Mr. Shelton. I'll pay again, but I want Martha back."

Shelton cleared his throat. He looked desperately at the bottle of whiskey beneath the desk. "Didn't Mr. Webster make everything clear to you?"

"Sammy I've known a long time. He talks too fast. I'll pay again. I've got the money with me. I want Martha back. I miss her, Mr. Shelton."

Shelton picked up the phone with a shaky hand and called Sam Webster.

"Mr. Webster, Charlie, you'd better come down to the hotel. There's a slight problem."

Sam Webster arrived in 20 minutes. He hardly noticed Slater. "What's up, Charlie?" he said. "Too many demands for 312? We'll raise the price again. Hell, weekends we should get five thousand. All the hotels raise the rates on weekends."

"It isn't that, Mr. Webster. It's Mr. Slater here; he has a problem."

Sam Webster turned to Walter Slater. "Wally, old boy," he said, "don't tell me you got someone else? A mistress, maybe? I'm surprised. I didn't figure you for a ladies' man. I'll tell you what, you're one of our first customers—the rates have gone up, but you don't have to go to the bottom of the list. Charlie here'll fix you up some night next week."

Walter Slater looked down at the floor. "You don't understand, Sammy, I don't have a mistress. I don't have anyone. It's Martha. I want her back, Sammy."

Sam Webster reached with automatic hand for the whiskey bottle. "Wally, what the hell is this! How am I gonna get her back? I told you the deal. We shook hands on it. Martha's gone. You're better off. Go out and find yourself a young one. What the hell can you care about Martha?"

"Sammy, she was my wife."

"Wife! What the hell, who needs it? I'm telling you, there's no way to bring her back." He turned to Shelton.

"Is there, Charlie?"

"I'm afraid not, Mr. Slater, there's just no way."

Walter Slater said nothing for a full minute. He watched Sam Webster drink the whiskey. Tears came to the corners of his sad eyes. "Sammy, if she's not home by tomorrow night, I'm going to the police."

"Wally, you're crazy. Go to the police. What will it do? They'll snoop around and they'll put you in the nuthouse. Who's gonna believe your story? There's no bodies. Without no bodies, the police can't do nothing."

"Tomorrow night, Sammy, I want Martha by tomorrow night." Walter Slater walked out of the hotel.

Sam Webster poured another glass of whiskey. "Can you imagine that guy? I can't believe it. That Martha was a horse. Nothing but a horse. I don't understand people anymore. Wally should kiss the ground I walk on and he wants to go to the police." He drank the whiskey. "Charlie, how many we got lined up?"

Shelton looked at his appointment book. "We're booked for almost three months."

"We're gonna have to raise the rates. I knew it. First of the month and the rates are going up."

The next evening, Walter Slater walked into the lobby of the Madison. Shelton was expecting him. Mr. Slater looked around as though he expected to see his wife. There was a tired look on his face.

"I'm sorry," Shelton said, "but there's nothing anyone can do."

Sam Webster came into the lobby. He was dressed in a dark suit. There was a white carnation in his buttonhole. He was smoking a huge cigar. He was swinging a walking stick with a solid-silver head. "How's everything going, Charlie, baby?" Sam hadn't noticed Walter Slater.

"Fine," Shelton said. "Mr. and Mrs. Cooper just checked in."

"Eddie Cooper we shoulda charged double. That **wife** of his, Susie, I know he'd pay a good ten grand to get rid of that pig."

Then Sam noticed Walter Slater. He slapped him hard on the back. "Wally, I tell you what. I'm taking you out with me tonight. I've got two blondes. They're acrobats. They'll make you forget old Martha."

"Sammy, I don't want no blonde acrobats. I want Martha." He was crying. Tears streaked his pale cheeks.

"Let me tell you something, Wally, I been patient with you. Now, I tell you what. You go to the police, go ahead. You're in this as much as we are. There's nothing you can do, anyway." Sam Webster puffed hard on his cigar. A cloud of gray smoke engulfed Walter Slater's face. "I tell you what, Wally, old boy, any more trouble out of you, I'm gonna hit you over the head and you spend the night in 312. That way, you might end up with Martha—and you might not. One more word, that's all, just one more word and you've had it. I'll lock you in the room. So, I blow a couple grand. I'm tired of seeing your crying face. Now, go ahead, say something."

Slater looked at Sam Webster in disbelief. He shook his head as though he were trying to remember something. He walked out of the hotel.

"Well, Charlie, old boy, how did I handle that?"

"You didn't mean it, did you, Mr. Webster?"

"Didn't mean what?"

"About locking Mr. Slater in 312?"

"Hell, yes, I meant it! You think I'm gonna let that creep ruin the best thing a guy ever had? I'd just as soon step on him. Who needs that kinda trouble?"

Shelton and Webster got through the spring and summer without any more client difficulties. Shelton had never realized there were so many people willing to pay so much money to have certain associates or dear ones disappear. Shelton had no idea how much money he had in the safe. Sam Webster was living like a king. He even bought a Rolls-Royce complete with chauffeur, and he was wearing flowers in his lapel every day. His name was in all the gossip columns, always mentioned along with some young actress or showgirl.

It was early fall, a clear September night, when the unpredictable happened. Shelton was drinking coffee out of his green Thermos when Sam Webster walked into the lobby. He was dressed in evening clothes, a flower in his lapel; and although he was carrying a half-full bottle of champagne, Shelton had never seen Sam Webster look so sober. "Charlie," he said, "I can't believe it. I just can't believe it."

"What happened, Mr. Webster?" Charlie said, sipping at his hot coffee and beginning to feel nervous for some reason.

"I was at the Grove Theater tonight with the acrobats. You know, the two blondes. A new show opened and I don't like to miss an opening. Well, we were sitting there in the first row enjoying the show. I was giving the chorus a thorough check—you know, in case there was anything extra-special—and I see *her* dancing in the line."

"See *who* dancing in the line, Mr. Webster?"

"Hilda! My Hilda, that's who!" Sam Webster was shouting. "Just like she looked thirty years ago!"

"Mr. Webster, that's not possible."

"Not possible! How can you say anything's not possible after the crazy things been going on around here? You telling Sam Webster that he doesn't know his own wife? I ain't never gonna forget that figure. Not the way it was thirty years ago. What do you think I married her for? Even the mole was there, right above her left knee. The same mole, in the same place. Charlie, it was Hilda, looking just like she did when I married her. Don't you see? Hilda always wanted to be a dancer. She always said she could've had a great career if she hadn't married me. That's what happened. We thought we were so smart. Those people that been disappearing from 312—don't you see, Charlie? Whatever they always dreamed about being in life—*that's the way they end up!* All Hilda ever talked about when we were first married was being a dancer. And now she's on her way; she's in the chorus line at the Grove Theater."

"You're sure it was Hilda, Mr. Webster?"

"Charlie, just like I'm standing here, I'm sure."

Sam Webster finished his champagne. Suddenly his face began to beam. His eyes came alive. He looked as if he might begin to jump up and down.

"Charlie, I've got it. Jesus Christ, I'm surprised I didn't think of it sooner. What the hell is the matter with me? I've got it, Charlie!"

"Got what, Mr. Webster?"

"Saturday's hero, that's what. Don't you see, I've always wanted to be a football hero. I can hear the roar of the crowd now. Those sunny fall afternoons and Sammy Webster, triple-threat back for Notre

Dame, is running wild on the gridiron. Goddamn."

"I don't understand, Mr. Webster."

"Don't understand! Charlie, all my life I've wanted to play football. When I was a kid, that's all I ever thought about. Only trouble was I couldn't play a lick. I used to sit in the stands and suffer. But now, Charlie, old boy, I can do it. I'm going to college. Notre Dame. I won't make all-American my sophomore year, just another sensational sophomore back, that's all. But my junior year, watch out! I'll be the talk of the country. No one is gonna stop Sammy Webster. Can't you see me fading back to throw one of my long touchdown bombs, the crowd going crazy, and the girls, Charlie, the girls, all those coeds. Those are real girls, Charlie, not freak acrobats. They'll all be screaming my name. Christ, I can hardly wait! Then about ten good years of pro ball. I'll develop my Webster bullet pass. Zip. Zip. Short, flat and hard, right over the line, no one'll be able to stop me. And once in a while, the Sammy Webster trademark, a high, soft one, right into the end zone. Charlie, goddamn it, I can't wait."

"Mr. Webster, you mean you're going to spend the night in Room 312?"

"Charlie, what the hell you think I been talking about? Who has the room reserved for tonight?"

Shelton looked at his appointment book. "Mr. and Mrs. Greenwald."

"You call that Greenwald and tell him he's been moved back a night. Tell him 312 has been closed for alterations. Tell him anything. I'm going home and get some sleep. I'll be back later tonight."

Sam Webster returned to the Hotel Madison shortly before midnight. Shelton could tell that he'd had a good sleep. He looked fresh and his eyes were clear. He was dressed in gray slacks and a soft gray sport shirt.

G. L. TASSONE   175

And, there was a pleasant odor of after-shave lotion about him.

"Well, Charlie," he said, "this is it. This is the big night. Did you call Greenwald?"

"Yes, sir. I moved him back a night."

"Good. I'm gonna miss you, Charlie. I'm sure gonna miss you."

"I'm gonna miss you, Mr. Webster."

Shelton got two paper cups and removed the whiskey bottle from beneath the desk. "Should we have one last farewell drink, Mr. Webster?"

"You go ahead, Charlie. I can't. I'm in training, you know. No one on the squad is allowed to drink."

Shelton poured some whiskey into a cup. Sam Webster had his eyes on the clock. "Well, Charlie, it's midnight straight up. I don't want to be late. It's all yours now, Charlie."

He put out his hand. The two men stood there shaking hands. "Thanks, Mr. Webster. I can hardly believe it."

"Goodbye, and don't forget to read the sports pages," Sam Webster said as he walked into the elevator. Shelton watched the elevator doors slide closed. The elevator started up.

"Goodbye, Mr. Webster," Shelton said to the empty lobby.

Sam Webster got out on the third floor. He walked down the dim corridor to Room 312. He turned the key in the lock and went into the dark room. He lay on the bed. He waited. Occasionally, he looked at the luminous dial on his watch. Football, coeds, crowds of screaming people were all busy in his head.

Suddenly, there was a blinding light and the loud blare of music. He was upright and he could feel his arms and legs moving. Finally, he could make out faces through a white glare of light. His arms and legs were still moving violently. There were attractive young men and women all around him. They were all dancing. He looked down at his feet. His young, handsome legs were keeping time to the music. He saw it all clearly. They were dancers. They were all dancing. Mr. Sam Webster was now dancing in the show at the Grove Theater.

The Golden Frog/ken w. purdy

The sergeant stood and held the door open for the other man.

"This is Lieutenant Simmons, Mr. Vanyon," he said. "I wonder would you just start over again and tell the lieutenant how this all happened?"

John Vanyon stood to shake hands. "Well, I suppose so," he said, "but after all, I just did tell you. . . ."

"I know, Mr. Vanyon," the sergeant said, "but I want the lieutenant to hear it from you yourself. You got to admit this is not any common thing. I mean, this is no traffic violation we're dealing with here. This is serious."

"Yes, I know," Vanyon said. "Very well." He dropped back into the chair. They were in a small office opening off the squad room. Their chairs were pulled up to a battered kitchen table. A coffeepot was going on an electric plate.

"You know who I am, I suppose?" Vanyon asked Lieutenant Simmons.

"I know your name, you're thirty-two, you're a professor of music at the University and you play the bells up there," Simmons said. "That's all I know."

"Assistant professor," Vanyon said. "And carillonneur. A carillon is a set of chromatically tuned bells hung in a tower, more than three octaves of them . . . well . . . in the summer, during vacation, I play three times a day, eight in the morning, noon, and nine at night. For the nine o'clock program I usually go into the tower about eight-thirty and practice for a while; we have a practice keyboard hooked up to xylophone bars instead of bells. I did that tonight. It was eight-thirty when I went in. The rain was beginning."

"Did you lock the door behind you?"

"I closed it," Vanyon said. "It locks itself; it has a spring latch. It swings very easily, for all its size. It's hung on ball-bearing hinges, I understand. I know it was locked. I heard the bolt slide into the slot. It has a slick, oil sound; you can't mistake it.

"I went up to the playing cabin in the top of the tower, and then. . . ."

"Excuse me," Simmons said. "I understand there's an elevator?"

"Yes, there's a small one in a corner of the tower," Vanyon said. "This is a bare tower; there's nothing inside it but the bells, a stairway and the elevator. The elevator is very slow, and as a rule I use the stairs."

"And the whole tower is about seven stories high?" Simmons said.

"Three hundred-odd feet."

"You must be in pretty good shape," Simmons said.

"I don't know," Vanyon said. "I suppose so."

"You must be strong," Simmons said.

"I noticed that when we shook hands," the sergeant said. "You got a strong grip."

"All carillonneurs have strong hands," Vanyon said. "The instrument does that. At any rate, I went up, and I ran through the program I intended to play. Then I climbed into the bell chamber—through a trap door in the ceiling of the cabin—and opened the louvers. I came down again and set up the clappers, something that must be done every time the instrument is played; it's a matter of adjustment. And at nine o'clock I began the program.

"You'll remember that it was at about nine that the storm really broke. I had been playing for about five minutes when the tower was hit. I understand it happens during almost every thunderstorm, but this was the first time I was there. I must say it was a fantastic sensation. There's a lot of noise attendant on playing the carillon. One's very close to the bells— and we have two that weigh seven tons each—and then there is a great clatter from the clapper wires, the wooden keys and so on. But when the lightning struck, I couldn't hear any of this over the tremendous crack the lightning bolt made.

"I kept on playing. I finished the program. I filed the music away, went up and closed the louvers, all the regular things. I put my shirt and jacket on, and then I discovered that the door wouldn't open."

"That's the door to the place upstairs, you mean?" Simmons said.

"Right. The playing cabin. I couldn't move it. I thought I must have locked it, absent-mindedly, but the latch was off. Still, I couldn't budge it. I thought of pulling the pins out of the hinges, but they were on the outside and I couldn't get at them. And the door itself is steel. It's painted to look like wood but it's steel."

"No phone in the tower?"

"No. And before tonight it had never occurred to me that there was any need for one. But I wasn't really bothered. After all, nothing much could happen to me. I decided that when the storm died down, I'd toll one of the big bells until someone came to the foot of the tower. Then I'd throw down the key to the main door, wrapped in a note, and wait for someone to come up and take the cabin door off its hinges.

"While I was waiting, I played something on the practice clavier. Then I played it on the bells, with the louvers closed, just for myself."

"What did you play?"

"It was Pleyel's *Sonata 3*," Vanyon said. "After that I played a Welsh round, and then I improvised for a while. I played until my hands were tired. When I stopped, I noticed that the thunder was barely audible. I opened one of the two windows. There was almost no rain falling. I looked down and that was when I first saw him. He was standing in the exact center of that little place in front of the door, in the center of the circle of light that falls there, and he was looking up. I waved and he waved back. I made a gesture to him to wait, and I ran over to the bench and scribbled the note, which you have now, and wrapped the key in it and tossed it to him. He caught it in one hand, and I remember thinking that it seemed very easy for him; he just stuck his hand out and took it. He read the note and then he moved out of sight. He went to the door."

"Now, why do you think he didn't open it?" Simmons said.

"For the reason he gave," Vanyon said. "He couldn't."

"But the sergeant says it opened right up for him," Simmons said.

"I know, and so did the cabin door. But you have to remember, that was some time later. My belief is that the lightning strike did it somehow—froze the doors to the jambs, both of them."

"Couldn't," the sergeant said.

"Well, I couldn't open mine, and he said he couldn't open the main door. I believed him, and I still think he was telling the truth."

"It's easier for you to believe some of this than it's going to be for me, I can tell you that," Simmons said.

"It's not a question of *belief*," Vanyon said. "Not for me, at least. I saw it all. I'm sure the sergeant has told you what happened next. He came out into the light again, waved in a kind of helpless way, clearly trying to indicate to me that the key wouldn't work, and then he walked over to the corner of the tower and began to climb it."

"A human fly," the sergeant said.

"Mr. Vanyon," Lieutenant Simmons said, "I know what that tower looks like, and I have to tell you right now that I find what you say hard to believe. All right, it's not perfectly smooth. Maybe there's a foothold here and there. *Here and there,* I say. But I think it would be a rough proposition to climb that tower even with a rope. Without a rope, I say it's impossible."

John Vanyon left them. He wrapped a handkerchief around the handle of the coffeepot and brought it to the table. They were shaking their heads. He filled his cup.

"Let it rattle," the sergeant said. "You can't chip *that* cup."

"Rattle?"

"Your hand was shaking a little when you poured the coffee."

"Was it?" Vanyon said. He carried the pot to its

stand. "Lieutenant Simmons," he said, "I suggest you just let me tell you what happened, straight through, and after that we can go over it and you can ask questions."

Simmons shrugged heavily. He smiled, his fat cheeks moving to slit his eyes. "Fine," he said. "But in that case I'd like to get a stenographer in here and take it down. Be much easier for us to go over it that way. You have no objection, have you?"

"No," Vanyon said. He didn't like the idea, but he couldn't think of an effective argument. He felt vaguely trapped, lightly but firmly held, like a man lost in a forest. The harshness of the room scratched on his nerves. He conceived that the two policemen across the table were implacably stupid and he had to hold down a rising hatred.

The sergeant got up and went out.

"That storm didn't cool things," Simmons said.

"Apparently not," Vanyon said.

"Do you play anything besides the—how do you say that—carillon?" Simmons said.

"Piano and organ. Most carillonneurs play one or the other."

"I took piano when I was a kid. It was a waste. When my wife wanted my kid to start, I told her nothing doing."

A tall girl came in. She was carrying a little black case, and the sergeant, behind her, his hand in the small of her back, lower than it needed to be, had another.

"Patrolwoman Tierney, Mr. Vanyon," he said.

She offered her hand. She was strong. Vanyon was six feet tall and she looked him level in the eye. She was made taller by red hair massed around her face,

the dense, wiry, incompressible kind of hair. The
lieutenant held a chair and she sat down without looking, a girl long used to having chairs held for her,
buttocks so firm that she seemed to touch the chair
in two small places only. She was a stenotypist and
when she had her little machine standing on its
bandy legs, she looked up and smiled.

"OK, Mr. Vanyon," Simmons said.

"He started up the tower," Vanyon said. "He was
on the corner, the southwest corner to be exact, so that
he had one foot and one hand on each wall. But only
for the first ten feet or so. Then he moved over to the
south wall. He came up fast, just incredibly fast. He
moved in a practiced way, a habitual way, as if he had
been up the tower before. He moved rhythmically. He
would reach for a handhold, and then a foothold;
he'd wait for a beat, then lift himself smoothly, reach,
wait, lift, reach, wait, lift—it was wonderful to watch.
He came right on up, and I could see him: young,
dark hair, tan, bareheaded, wearing a trench coat. He
looked up and grinned at me. He had very white teeth,
or perhaps they just looked white because he was so
tan. He came up to the window and hooked his elbows
over the sill. He had an engaging, open look, and he
seemed young except that his nose had been broken,
more than once, too.

" 'Well,' he said, 'are you asking me in?'

"I laughed. 'You've come all this way, why not?' I
said.

"He came over the sill and stood in the middle of
the floor, soaking wet. 'I suppose that's the stuck door,'
he said, 'since it's the only one in the place.' He gave
it a shake. 'Buggered,' he said, 'just like the one below.'

"I introduced myself and he said his name was

Dennis Rolt. He didn't say more. Judging from his age, I took him to be a graduate student or an instructor. I wasn't surprised at not having seen him before. When ten thousand students are set down in a city of this size. . . . I asked him where in the world he had learned to climb.

" 'In England,' he said. 'In my school everybody ran up and down the buildings like so many deathwatch beetles. One can't do anything with really modern buildings, of course, but anything old, or anything fake-Gothic, like this, is easy enough. Might as well have ladders running up them. They take in the ladders going down, though. Different matter, going down.'

" 'Easy or not,' I told him, 'it was very good of you to come up, and. . . .' I stopped there, and he laughed.

" 'You don't really know why I *did* come up, do you?' he said.

"And I didn't, you know.

" 'I could hardly expect to open your door if you could not,' he said, 'and in any case, it wouldn't get you out if I could, because the one below's jammed as well. So I didn't come up to rescue you. You can be bloody sure I'm not going to offer to carry you down the wall on my back.'

" 'You're right about that,' I said. 'I wouldn't go at the point of a gun.'

" 'And I didn't come to keep you company,' he said. 'You change ringers know you're going to be lonely when you sign on.'

" 'Carillonneurs,' I told him. 'Change ringers are something else again.'

" 'It's all bells,' Rolt said. 'And balls to all bells, I say. It's a dreadful kind of music. And balls to all music, comes to that, bells or no bells. But that's not to say a word against musicians. Musicians I'm for. Musicians of all kinds and stripes, players of the lute, the pipes, the mouth harp, the pianoforte, the musical saw, the fiddle and the flute. Also all artists of whatever kind, from Leonardo to Bernard Buffet; painters in oil, water color, *gouache,* buttermilk, egg yolk, India ink or stale beer; painters on canvas, linen, silk, ivory, wet plaster and sidewalks; also engravers, masters of mezzotint or whatever; Lord's Prayer pinhead specialists; money-makers, particularly French money-makers; sculptors, whether of stone, marble, jade, clay or ice for carnivals —all sculptors, particularly, in my view, untutored Eskimo sculptors sawing away on whaletooth and soap-stone; some jewelers, bookbinders, *chefs de cuisine;* one *chef d'équipe;* three unicycle riders and a very few bill collectors. All those, and a good many more, and emphatically I am including all carillonneurs and bell bongers, whether of the high degree, the middle or the low.'

"He walked up and down the cabin, very fast, as he talked," Vanyon said, "and first I thought he was drunk and then that he was psychotic—crazy. And the more he talked, the more he did talk. His articula-tion fed on itself. I would like to have had Miss Tierney there to record it, because I can't begin to reproduce it."

Patrolwoman Tierney smiled, enough to suggest that she appreciated the mild compliment, not enough to suggest that she thought it a jolly idea.

" 'I came up,' Rolt said, 'because you represent the ideal human person. It was perfectly evident, even when who knows how many furlongs stood on end separated us, that you were among the ideal human persons for my purposes, or purpose, because really I have only one. You are an artist, a perceiving, intelligent individual; you are marooned and helpless, locked up, tied, tossled, confined, wrapped and fastened, lonely and willing to listen. What more could a salesman want? And that's what I am, a salesman, a salesman on what I like to think is the highest level: a doctrinal salesman. I sell doctrine. I am the only man in the world who can give you, fully and cogently, the doctrine of The Golden Frog. Oh, there are others —all of them taught by me, mark you—who can explain it around the edges, give you the soup and salad of it, so to speak, and maybe the cheese and coffee, but for the heart of the matter, the entree, the *boeuf Massoni*, I have to do that myself. And it's not often that I have the chance. It won't do for just anyone. I have to select, and select, and select again, and even then I'm often wrong. I was perfectly prepared, you know, when I climbed in that window, to find that I'd been wrong again, and that I'd have to sit here, mute and helpless, and let you rant and rave over me about bells, bore me until my skull bones melted and ran hot out of my ears, and I was ready to pay the price, and God knows I loathe hearing other people talk. But I was *not* wrong; I was right, and I shall tell you everything.

" 'The Golden Frog is, naturally, not a frog at all, but a tree toad, the common *Hyla versicolor-versicolor.* Being *called* a frog, if he were actually a frog, he would be of no use. He is *Hyla versicolor-versicolor,* and if you don't know what he looks like, he looks like this.'

"Rolt opened his hand and held it out, and there in his palm was a tiny golden toad, as big as a quarter, perhaps, smooth and old-looking.

" 'The Golden Frog,' he said, 'is a god; naturally you'll have guessed that. Where he stands in the pantechnicon of gods I know, of course, but I cannot tell you—not yet, not yet. Mind you, I don't say he is

God. Mind you, I don't say he is not. He is The Golden Frog. You are bright, you are clever, you are no fool, the insane chatter of your bell clappers hasn't beaten the wits out of you, no, and not even the lightning bolts rattling on your rooftree here one to the minute —do you know I saw your blasted tower hit ten times tonight if it was hit once? But you're bright, and you know that *Hyla versicolor-versicolor* is the tree toad, if only because I've told you so, and you know that the tree toad is a limpet thing and climbs verticals and hangs to walls and likes high places, and you'll have connected that, won't you, with me coming up the tower? And have you connected it with you *being* up the tower, though you came up, Lord knows, in a clot's fashion, jiggling on the end of a wire in an elevator, bouncing on a string like a yo-yo. Still, you are here; here you are, up.

" 'Nothing. He does nothing, The Golden Frog, and *that's* what he's for. It's for us to do, don't you see? The Golden Frog will not make *my* winter rye grow forty-seven hundred feet higher than yours, no, nor a Persian inch higher; he doesn't know if a sparrow falls, and he doesn't care. Since he will not catch you falling, he won't let you go, either, and that's a simple concept which I'm sure you grasp. Let me tell you what happened to me one time: I was rock climbing, in a manner of speaking; I was going up the south face of the Gerrsgarten, and alone. This was before I lived in The Frog, and I was a devotee of the cult of Barquah; indeed, for a long time I thought that everyone born during October of 1932 was a *Barquahniste*. As you know, either now or because I'm telling you, Barquah had fifteen thousand male children, each of whom was a *nark*, or holy man, fully capable of those inexplicable actions we are pleased to call miracles.

" 'Now, my natal *nark* was Tu'bip Alem, and it was upon Tu'bip Alem that I always called when I needed help, which was often enough, Lord knows. And when that bloody *piton* pulled—I saw it pulling; the crack seemed to open, widen, and something or somebody inside the mountain pushed it out—and I fell, I yelled, you can imagine, for Tu'bip Alem to help me. And I had time to yell. That's a five-thousand-meter drop, off the crest of the south face at Gerrsgarten. Oh, I yelled. And a great brown hand came down out of the clouds and caught me and held me. And a tremendous, booming voice, a voice that was the topmost end, the double-distilled distillate of every booming baritone voice since time first whispered, this great voice boomed out and said in Gjindi, "Do you call Tu'bip Alem or Tu'bip Alam?" Now, as I have said, Tu'bip Alem was my natal *nark*, while Tu'bip Alam was just another of the fifteen thousand to me, although no doubt very important to those whose natal *nark* he was, and to *shatusa* herders, whose patron he was, but still nothing to me. But which had caught me? How could I tell in whose big brown hand I lay? I tried to think for a split second, and the hand tightened and began to crush me. So I made the decision on an ethical basis: Honesty is the best policy. "I called," I said, "on Tu'bip Alem." The great brown hand opened, and slowly, slowly turned and dropped me. It was the hand of Tu'bip Alam, and I was no *shatusa* herder.'

"I interrupted him," Vanyon said. "I told him I had heard that story before, years before. It's an old gag, I told him. Usually you hear it told about St. Francis and St. Francis of Assisi.

"He laughed. 'I don't doubt it,' he said. 'But you only *heard* it. It *happened* to *me*!' "

"Did you believe him?" Simmons said.

"I don't know," Vanyon said. "And it doesn't matter, because, don't you see, you must see, the important thing was not whether what he was saying was true or not, the important thing was that he was saying it. It wasn't important that the gold frog might be a god; it *was* important that he obviously did believe that it was a god. To me Dennis Rolt was a wonder, he was a free spirit, he was the voice of the world as we would like to think the world should be, a paradise of astonishment and beauty. Just to hear him made me feel that everything in my own life, or almost everything, was dull and hopeless. And that in spite of the fact that I thought, as I told you before, that he might be crazy, completely mad. No one could hear a man talk as he talked without wondering if he were sane, but still. . . ."

"You say he made you feel that your life was dull," Simmons said. "You were jealous of him?"

"Oh, yes, I suppose I was," Vanyon said, "although that's a very crude way of putting it."

"That's why you killed him?" the sergeant said softly. "Because you were jealous of him?"

Vanyon turned. "When I first saw you, sergeant," he said, "I decided you were a stupid man. I was wrong. You aren't just stupid. You're a monument to stupidity. In you, stupidity burrows to a brand-new low. You are. . . ."

"You better watch your mouth, buddy," Simmons interrupted.

The sergeant's face was burning red and his right hand twitched rhythmically and convulsively on his thigh.

"He'd better watch his," Vanyon said.

"Turn it off," Simmons said. "Get on with your

story. What was the last thing he said, Tierney, before this fuss?"

Patrolwoman Tierney lifted a few accordion folds of paper from her machine's little trough.

" 'Just to hear him made me feel that everything in my own life, or almost everything, was dull and hopeless,' " she read.

"He went on with the story," Vanyon said. "My cutting in about St. Francis didn't stop him.

" 'There I was,' he said, 'dropping like a stone down the face of the Gerrsgarten, spurned by the great brown hand of Tu'bip Alam. It didn't matter. I was saved by another means, which is not important. In point of fact, to quiet any absurd skepticism that might rise in you, or, rather, any *additional* and absurd skepticism that might rise in you, I will say that I was saved by bloody chance: I fell into a snowfield, twenty ruddy inches of fresh powder hanging on the steepest slope in the Alpes-Maritimes, rolled about a kilometer and came out, nine-tenths suffocated but alive and with the seat in my pants, just above the village of Voiten, and within sight of the bar run by the Dutchman Glauvert, and that was where I told the story for the first time, and that was where I left Barquah, for good. Or for bad, who'm I to say?'

"I interrupted him," Vanyon said. "I said, 'What do you do now, when you're not running up rock faces or bell towers?'

" 'I roam about,' he said. 'I roam about, and earn vast sums of money in ways that would dazzle you, and I make love to all the girls who will have me, and some that won't, too, if I think they have the understanding to be truly grateful afterward, and when people will listen I tell them of The Frog. I have carried the doctrine of The Frog to odd places: Parlakimedi, which you know, if only because I'm telling you so, is in Madras, and Pin Hook, which I suppose everyone knows is in Indiana. I tell them of The Frog, the All-Knowing and All-Seeing and Do-Nothing Frog who is the ultimate solution of our *mille*-faceted problems. What is the doctrine of The Frog, you say, and I say, the doctrine of The Frog is, Send not for any other man to do, lest you be done, and ever since *For Whom the Bell Tolls* was published, a pretty pun has been possible on that sentence, and even before that time it was possible, for a man learned in the literature of the English language, to make and enjoy this pun on *done*. As Andrew Salter so often says in private conversation, "Why aren't you laughing? You aren't laughing enough!" but to be serious, you will concede that although The Frog speaks only once, he speaks with sheer eloquence and with the voice of wisdom beyond plumbing, and if you are reminded of Churchill bare-breasted on the beaches in 1939, congratulations to you, but you have misread me. I say again, The Frog is wise beyond wisdom, for there is no answer beyond his answer, which is, Do, lest you be Done. Or, reduced, Do. This is all wisdom, boiled down, in the great black kettle of the other sky, the one *beneath* us, to one drop, one syllable, Do, and *Hyla versicolor-versicolor,* when he cries, "Wh'dee! Wh'dee!" cries "Do!" in all the languages, or nearly all, of the whole Melanee group, as I'm sure you know, if for no other reason than that I'm telling you so.

" 'Join us, then, in The Frog. Carry the voice of The Frog to a supine, passive, limp, flaccid, custardy world full, like seeds in a jam pot, of people being done, not doing. Say you'll come, and when you do then I'll tell you what it is to have life in The Golden Frog, where we live in The Frog, and I'll tell you a good many other things that will amaze and startle you and rouse you until your brain bubbles like so much porridge, and your blood will run till you hear it screaming down your arteries and up your veins, and if you stick a pin in your arm, the stuff will bore a hole through the ceiling and just *that* will get you off; we call it Reverse Medicine and when you live in The Frog you need no other, and what is more. . . .'

"It was about there," Vanyon said, "that he gave the door another jerk, in passing as it were, and it opened. We were both amazed, but there it was, swinging open.

" 'All right!' Rolt said. 'What's good for one's good for the other, and it's even money the one below is cured as well.' We didn't know about that, but certainly the cabin door was free. I still think, and he did, too, that the lightning strike had something to do with their sticking.

"At any rate, I said to Rolt, 'We'll go down and look and if it's open, I'll buy the drinks.' But he said, 'The bit about the drinks is all right, but I'll go the way I came.' And he went over to the window and moved out of it backward. He hung there for a second, his elbows hooked on the sill, just as he had when he came in, and then he levered himself out and down. I remembered what he'd said about the ladders being taken in going down, and I wanted to talk him into coming down with me on the stairs, and I suppose he knew it because he said, 'Stairs are for clots, but don't worry, The Frog will soon unclot you.' He moved differently going down, much more slowly, and not at all rhythmically. I watched, looking down at him. I really don't believe he had made ten feet, and certainly it wasn't fifteen, before he fell. I saw it all very clearly. His right foot came loose and the sudden weight transfer jerked his right arm loose; I heard the fingernails of his left hand scrabble and grate on the granite and then he went, out backward, looking up, all of a piece, exactly like a man going off a high board, and instantly there was a great shout, 'Tu'bip Alem, save me!' and because he was now falling so fast, the sound was altered by the Doppler effect, you know, as when one hears the tone of a crossing bell change when one's riding in a train, and the 'save me!' was stretched out, dropping, 'say-ay-ayve-meeee!' and then he hit."

Miss Tierney's machine clicked briefly as she caught up. The coffee bubbled.

"I will say one thing," Lieutenant Simmons said. "In twenty-two years on the Force, and ten in Homicide, that is the damnedest story I ever sat down to listen to. The damnedest."

"Look, Mr. Vanyon," the sergeant said. "Now, look. Here is this fellow falling three hundred feet and he knows he's going to be dead in two seconds and he yells out that Tubepalum or whatever. Why? If he's going to yell anything, for some heathen saint to save him, and he's just through telling you he doesn't believe in *that* one . . . my point is, why didn't he yell for the tree toad, the gold frog?"

"He was making a joke," Vanyon said.

"A joke? A *joke*?" Simmons said. "The man's two seconds from a messy end, and he's making a joke? In mid-air?"

"I think so," Vanyon said. "I think he was saying to me, 'You know that when a man's dying he often reverts to the belief he was brought up in. But I'm doing this consciously, and satirically, and laughing, to show you that for me it's still The Frog!' "

Simmons looked at the sergeant, who was looking at him. The lieutenant's head inclined toward the door and they rose as one and left without a word.

Patrolwoman Tierney's hands were folded in her pretty lap. Since she'd stopped working her machine, she had been staring at Vanyon with interest. Where this interest rose, what spurred it, how deeply it ran, he could not know.

"I have an idea they didn't believe me," he said. He didn't see great profit in offering her this opening, but the silence and her straight-line regard had become oppressive.

"Not a word," she said. "Nor did I."

You are a dumb bitch, Vanyon said to himself. "It was as near the truth as I could make it," he said.

"Nobody in the room believed it but you, then," she said. She laughed. "I think the sergeant and the lieutenant are only wondering how to go about asking you some questions about it."

She was right.

"Oh, there's no doubt about that at all," Simmons was saying. "He threw the fella out the window on his head and that's for sure. The question is why he did it and how we can get it out of him. You asked him why we couldn't find the gold toad he says Rolt had?"

"I asked him," the sergeant said. "The body was so near clean, you know. The two hundred-odd dollars, and not another thing, not a wallet, not a letter, not so much as a laundry ticket, and no gold toad, either. He said it must have fallen out of Rolt's pocket on the way down, and it was either lost in the grass or buried under him, or somebody picked it up before the squad car got there."

"Doesn't the dumb bastard know that the toad being missing ruins his story?"

"I told him that. I told him if we had the toad there'd be a different face on the matter. He said if we had the toad it would wind up on some alderman's watch charm, but it didn't matter because it was lost and nobody had it."

"He deny he was the first man to the body?"

"Oh, no. He admitted that. He ran down the stairs, the door opened all nice and proper and he went out."

"That door business. That takes brass, a lie like that."

"It does. Well, lieutenant, with all respect, I got to say that you and I are a poor bet to get anywhere arguing with this joker. The old way is the best way, I always say, and an hour would do it, too, with this one. He'd cave in in a hurry, this one would."

"I believe you. But there's hell to pay if you get caught working over any of these eggheads. This is no bum from West Ninth Street. You let a college professor trip and fall against the wall a couple of times and you're liable to get hauled up in front of Congress. 'Gestapo' is what they'll call you. You'll get famous on television."

" 'Cossack' I like better than 'Gestapo,' " the sergeant said, "and I been called both. Look, he's got to prove it, right? I give you my word, I won't put a mark on him, and I'll have him dictating a statement in thirty minutes flat."

"I have to go upstairs and see McGuire," the lieutenant said. "I don't know anything about anything."

"That's OK with me," the sergeant said. He walked briskly from the room.

"Mr. Vanyon," he said, "will you just come with me? Will you come, too, Tierney?"

Miss Tierney smiled with what seemed to Vanyon to be real warmth. "Of course," she said.

• • •

It was an hour later, or an hour and a bit, and by no chance, that Lieutenant Simmons saw Patrolwoman Tierney coming up the stairs. She was carrying the tools of her trade. She was ever so little damp, as if someone had blown at her head through a Japanese flower wetter, the kind that makes a mist.

"Well?" Simmons said.

"Not a word out of him," she said. "Tom tried everything he could, and I tried a couple of things, and we tried a couple together, but it was no go. Of course, we were being careful of the bastard, but even so, he should have caved in. He didn't. The man came up the wall, he says, and fell off of it."

"Where's Vanyon now?" Simmons said.

"Tom's putting his clothes on him," Miss Tierney said. "He's all right. He can't walk, he's swollen in a couple of places, but by morning he'll be OK."

Simmons saw him in the morning.

"You know what happened to me?" Vanyon said.

"Nothing happened to you," Simmons said. "But something will if you open your big yap. Two things will happen to you. First, you'll get arrested if you spit on the sidewalk, and you'll get arrested if you don't. Second, you'll have an accident, and nothing trivial, either. So shut up. You killed a man!"

"You know goddamned well I didn't."

"You did. And you look like you're getting away with it, for the time being, and maybe for longer, although that I doubt. But nothing happened to you, and you'll do well to remember it. You can pick up your hat and get out of here, and they'll tell you at the desk where you can go and where you can't, pending the inquest and so on and so on."

Vanyon looked around for Patrolwoman Tierney

on his way through the station house to the street, but he was not really sure he wanted to see her again, ever. Crouching naked to her ingenuity and the sergeant's iron-hard brutality, he had been frightened almost beyond endurance, so that he wondered why consciousness did not leave him. He had endured what they did only because he had no alternative: He was not completely craven and so he could not or would not put an end to the agony by saying he had killed Rolt when he had not; there was no other door he could open. Not much later on, he would be able to convince himself that he had maintained his will against theirs because he was standing in the light that Dennis Rolt had cast, standing in the reflected glow of The Frog. For now, it was enough to think that the red-haired girl and the dough-faced sergeant had martyred him, but left him living. In fact, he thought, if Rolt was the prophet, what might Vanyon be?

The eight o'clock program of that morning was the first he had missed in a long time, and he felt bad about it, as if the fault were somehow his. He was on the street at a little after 11 and he took a taxi to the tower. Two groundkeepers were setting squares of turf at the foot of the tower, and 30 or 40 students were watching them. Nobody recognized Vanyon and he was quick with the door. He threw the inner bolt, something he had never done before, and looked carefully around. He got into the elevator cab and pushed the top button. He was lifted slowly up the damp inner wall, in silence except for the whine of the electric motor and its gears high above. He swung the playing-cabin door to and fro. It did not seem to be free and easy in the jamb, as he remembered it, neither did it stick. He left it open. It was hard for him to climb the short ladder to the bell chamber, but he made it. When he had opened one set of louvers, he realized that he was so sore and stiff he would not be able to play, and he closed them again as soon as he was sure that there was no one hiding in the dark places behind the bells. He crawled back down the ladder. He sat on the bench where he had been sitting the night before watching Rolt storm to and fro, and it was easy for him to think that the mad and tantalizing torrent of the dead man's words still rang in the room. Sometimes, in the bell chamber, he would touch the rim of a bell with a half dollar, to hear the hum of it run on until you couldn't be sure if the sound had ended or not, and he thought he could hear Rolt's voice in the same way. He sat in the playing cabin for a long time. Going down in the elevator, he looked carefully all around. At the door he turned out the lights. The windows in the tower were narrow, they were archers' slits, really, the lowest of them 30 feet from the ground. No one could see him. He went to the corner of the tower farthest from the elevator, where the steam pipes came through the floor. He knelt there for a moment, then moved to the center of the floor where a shaft of light angled down. He opened his hand and looked at the little frog he had lifted from its hiding place behind the cluster of pipes. It was heavy and smooth and golden. He had it now, and he would keep it. It lay heavy on his hand, so heavy, so solid that it seemed a part of him. He remembered, he believed, every word Rolt had spoken, and it was easy for him to recall the two places where Rolt said he had been: Pin Hook, Indiana, and Parlakimedi in Madras. "I have carried the doctrine of The Frog to odd places. . . ." He dropped the rounded lump of gold into a pocket of his jacket. He unlatched the door and went out. The groundkeepers had finished their work, and the students had gone away. A hot sun hung in a windless sky. He turned to look at the tower. He knew that he would never see it again, that he would never come back to it.

The Annex/john d. mac donald

During the last hour of the night, the charge nurse looked in at the critical in Room 11, intensive-care section, coronary. She scowled and made an ugly, displeased mouth and hastened to replace the dislodged I. V. needle in the vein inside the elbow of the right arm, immobilized by the straps, the board and the side rail of the bed. She checked the glucose drip, made a small adjustment of the flow valve, checked oxygen supply, listened to the ragged labor of the pulse and went off and found the pretty little special drinking coffee in the treatment room and joking with the redheaded intern.

After chewing her out with a cold expertise that welled tears into the blue eyes, she herded her back to her night watch over the patient.

"I wasn't gone three minutes, honest," she said.

"An hour before dawn they get restless," the charge nurse said. "As if they had someplace to go, some appointment to keep."

• • •

When the first gray light of the morning made the shape of the window visible, he dressed quickly and went out. He guessed that they would not be expecting him to leave that room so soon after arriving.

There were shadows of night still remaining in the empty streets, so that even though he knew his way and walked swiftly, the city seemed strange to him. They were changing it so quickly these past few years. The eye becomes accustomed to the shape and bulk of structures, giving them only a marginal attention; yet when, so abruptly, they were gone, one had the feeling of having made a wrong turn somewhere. Then even the unchanged things began to look half strange.

He turned a dark corner and saw the hotel lights in the distance. A taxi came swiftly to the cross-town corner, made a wrenching, shuddering turn and sped up the empty avenue, and he caught a silhouette glimpse of the sailboat hats of nuns in the dark interior, two or three of them.

He had not been in the hotel for years. He saw at once that it was quite changed. That certain quaintness of the lobby that once set off the high style of the moneyed people and the women of the theater was now merely a shabbiness. He realized that he could have guessed it, because were it not changed, they would not be mixed up in this sort of thing. And his shabby assignment in an unknown room would have occurred in some other place, perhaps even in another city at another time.

There was no one behind the desk. He felt in his pocket for the identification he would have to present and felt fear and irritation when he did not find it at once. Then, among coins, he fingered the shape of it and took it out and held it in his clasped hand. As he wondered whether to tap the desk bell, he saw movement out of the side of his eye and turned and saw a man walking toward him out of the lobby shadows.

"Mr. Davis?" the small man said; and as he came into the light, his face was elusively familiar. He searched memory and finally recalled the image of the same face, a bellhop uniform in dull red and gray, big brass circle of the master key ring looped around the scrawny neck. And the name came back.

"Do you remember me, Leo? From before?"

"Sure," the man said. He leaned against the desk and yawned. Davis knew the man did not remember him at all.

"You're the manager now?"

"So they keep telling me."

"Come up in the world, eh?"

"I guess so." He yawned again. "You got that thing?"

He felt unaccountably shy about revealing what they had given him. He said, "I keep telling them that they should use ordinary things. But they get fanciful. It just makes everything harder to explain when things go wrong. What kind of a sentimental nut would have a gold miniature of his own dog tag made? A grown man is supposed to get over being in a war."

"Look, I have to see it." Leo's tone was patient and bored, and Davis knew the man had no interest in what he thought and very little interest in why he had come here.

He held his hand out and the little wafer gleamed on his open palm. Leo took it, glanced at it and put it in his own pocket.

"They didn't tell me you'd keep it."

"The room you want is four-two-four-two."

"Are you supposed to keep it? Did they make that clear?"

"Forty-two forty-two. Four thousand, two hundred and forty-two, Mr. Davis. OK?"

"All right. I'll assume you're supposed to keep it, Leo. It's their problem, not mine. But you're supposed to turn over the key. I know *that*."

"I can't, buddy, because the only keys here are the keys to the main house here. You should know that and they should know that. Right? What we're talking about is the annex. Which is being torn down."

"Then there isn't anybody in it?"

"Did I say that, mister? Did anybody say that?"

"There's no reason to get ugly about it, Leo."

"Who's ugly? Listen, they got old foops in there living there since the year one, and lease agreements and all that stuff, so about the only thing they can do is work around them until they get sick of all the noise and mess and get out. There aren't many left now. I think maybe your party is the only one left on that floor, but I don't keep close track. I've got enough to do here without worrying about over there."

"So what do I do about a key? Am I supposed to go knock on the door, for God's sake?"

"Mrs. Dorn is over there. She's got a master key to the whole annex."

"Does she know about me?"

"Why should she? Just con her a little, Mr. Davis. Play it by ear. OK?"

"I don't have much choice, I guess."

"Has anybody lately? Come this way."

Leo led the way back through the lobby and through a huge empty kitchen, where night lights picked up the gleam and shape of stainless-steel racks and tables.

He pulled a door open and turned on a weak bulb at the head of a narrow flight of stairs.

"The regular way over there has been boarded up, so what you do is just follow the way the red pipe runs along the ceiling there, and when you come to the stairs finally, go on up and you'll find her around someplace."

Three steps down, he turned to say his thanks in some massively sarcastic way; but as he turned, the door was slammed. There were distant lights in the vast reaches of the basement, just enough for him to make out the red pipe suspended by straps from the low ceiling overhead. There was a sweaty dampness in the basement. In some far corner, a laboring machine was making a slow and heavy chuffing sound. It made a vibration he could feel through the soles of his shoes as he walked. He noticed that the red pipe overhead was of some kind of plastic material, sufficiently flexible so that there was a perceptible expansion and contraction as the machine made its thick and rhythmic sound.

He estimated that he had walked more than a city block before he came to the stairs, where the red pipe disappeared into a wall. These were unexpectedly wide and elegant stairs, marble streaked with gray and green, ascending in a gentle curve. At the top of the stairs, he pushed a dark door open and found himself in an enormous lobby. It had the silence of a museum. Dropcloths covered the shapes of furniture. Plaster dust was gritty on the floor. Some huge beams had fallen and were propped at an angle, as in pictures of bombings.

"Mrs. Dorn!" he called. "Mrs. Dorn!" The sound did not seem to carry. It died at once into the silence.

Then he heard a click-tock of high heels and he

could not tell where the sound was coming from. "Yes?" she said. "You, there! Up here!" Her voice was musical; the tone, impatient. He looked up and saw her standing at the broad ornate railing of a mezzanine floor, looking down at him, in silhouette against a window beyond her. "Yes? What do you want?"

"Can I speak to you a minute?"

"I'm very busy. Well . . . come on up."

She turned away. He looked around and saw the stairs and went up. There was a library and writing room at the top of the stairs. Several doors opened from the room. He tried them, one by one, and found they opened onto corridors. Then, close behind him, she chuckled and, as he turned, startled, she said, "It's really very confusing. I used to get hopelessly lost when I first came here."

She looked like someone he had known, somewhere, perhaps a long time ago. She had a soft and pretty face, dark wings of careless hair, and she looked at him in a familiar and mocking way of old secrets shared. She wore a shift of some tweedy gray substance over a young, sturdy body with a vital heft of hip and weight of breast.

"I wonder, Mrs. Dorn, if you could——"

"Just a moment, please. I missed this room somehow, and the crews will be arriving any minute, and it would be just my rotten luck if they started here, wouldn't it?" She began to walk slowly around the room, pausing from time to time to hold at arm's length a piece of soft yellow chalk in the measuring gesture of the artist. She nodded to herself from time to time and would mark with the chalk a piece of paneling, or a chair, or the frame of an old painting.

At last she sighed and turned toward him with a smile of enduring patience.

"Done, I guess. As well as I can do it, anyway. They don't really give a damn about saving anything. You have to watch them like hawks. They'll pretend they didn't see the mark and smash stuff to powder and then look so *terribly* innocent. They hate old things, I guess. And hate the loveliest old things worst of all. They just want to come in and biff, bang, crunch and truck it away—get it over with and on to the next job. My, how they resent me, and having to save things and handle them gently and take them to our warehouse. You wouldn't believe it."

The mark she made each time was a *D* with a cross drawn through it, like a cancellation.

"What did you want?" she asked.

"They told me that you're the one to see. You can lend me the master key."

"Really? And exactly what room do you want to get into? And why?"

"Four-two-four . . . oh. Forty-two forty. It will take only a . . . very few minutes."

"On the forty-second floor. Now isn't that quaint! Isn't that the living end!"

"What's so funny, Mrs. Dorn? I don't think anything is particularly funny."

"I couldn't possibly explain it to you. I'll have to show you."

"You could let me take the key, couldn't you?"

"My dear man, so much has been torn down and thrown away and smashed, you could wander around up there for weeks trying to find a way to the right floor and the right wing. Even if I believed you, I'd have to go with you in any case."

She led the way back down and through the silence of the lobby and to a back corridor, and into a birdcage elevator no more than five feet square. She reached and clanged the door shut, turned a worn brass handle and they began to creak slowly upward. He stared up through the ceiling of woven metal strips and saw the sway of the moving cables and, far overhead, a pale square of gray sky.

The animation and mocking amusement had gone out of her. She leaned, sagging, looking downward, finger tips on the brass lever, and he sensed that he had no part in what she was thinking. He could look at her with that feeling of invasion one has in watching someone sleep. There was a small mole below the corner of her mouth, on the pale concavity below the soft weight of her underlip. Her lashes were long and dark. He saw the lift and fall of her slow breathing and was aware of a warmth and scent of her breath. There were two deep pockets in the gray shift. The master key would have to be in one or the other. So it could be done. There was always a way.

Suddenly he had the feeling he was being trapped in some curious way, was being led from his assignment into a plan devised for some other reason, a plan wherein his role was minor; and looking at the panel above her resting hand, he saw what had probably given him subtle warning. There were brass buttons for the floors, pressed so many hundred thousand times the incised digits were almost worn away; yet when the gray light struck them properly, he could make out the topmost numeral of the vertical row—21.

"So that's it." he said. "That's very funny." He made his mouth stretch wide in the knowing grin. The girl looked at him, startled and puzzled. "There's no forty-second floor," he said.

Frowning, she turned and looked at the row of

buttons and then back at him. "You're serious? Don't you know about the annex at all? You know how the transients are. Top floor. Top floor. It's all they can think about. But the people who stay have to have private lives, don't they? Not all cluttered up with salesmen and people coming to town for the theater and all that. You've never been in the business, have you? All the city hotels are just the same, you know. The elevators for the transients go only so high, just to such and such a number, and the quiet floors, where people live, are above that, always, and they have their private ways to get up to them."

She was so very patient that he felt ashamed of accusing her and felt irritated with himself for not having guessed, long ago, what she told him. There had always been enough clues. There were always people going through the hotel lobbies, looking neither right nor left, walking by the regular elevators to some special place and service awaiting them.

But when the elevator stopped and they got out, she reached back into it, pressed the lowest button, yanked her arm out quickly and slammed the latticework door. It began to creak downward, with a clicking of pulleys and rasp of cables. She looked up at him and wrinkled her nose in mischief and mockery, saying, "Don't look so worried. There'll be other ways down." He remembered that she had not told him the joke, and he was once again annoyed at her.

These were broad corridors, pale gray, with composition floors, lighted by misted glass panels set into the ceiling. He tried to walk beside her, but she kept quickening her pace, and he realized she wanted him to walk behind her, a person guided rather than a companion. Many times they reached an intersection where the corridors stretched for vast distances, and sometimes she would pause to orient herself and then turn confidently right or left.

He noticed that all the numbers had been taken off the doors. He could see the raw holes where they had been screwed through gray paint into the plywood.

She was 15 feet ahead of him, the dark hair bouncing at the nape of her neck to her swift, buoyant stride. The coarse gray fabric pulled in alternating diagonal tensions against her rear, and somehow he knew that were she quite still and quite bare, were he to place his hands so that his finger tips were hooked around the shelf of hip socket, feeling the warm, smooth slide of membrane over bone, holding her from the rear, his hands placed as a player holds a basketball for the long set shot, then through some delicious coincidence of design, the pads of his thumbs would fit precisely into the two deep dimples spaced below her spine. He shook himself out of the erotic musing, remembering how often they had told him that assignments were mishandled too often for exactly this reason.

At the end of a corridor, she pulled a heavy fire door open and turned to give him a bawdy wink, to run her tonguetip across her lips, as though she had read his mind and his weakness; and he determined not to look at her as she climbed the stairs ahead of him, and looked instead at the steel treads set into the concrete. He lost track of the number of flights they climbed. It winded him; and when he helped her push another fire door open, he tried to conceal his laboring lungs and to seem as fresh as she.

These corridors were a pale yellow, like weak winter sunlight, and at last they came to a small elevator standing open. The fluorescence inside was harsh and there was a sharp minty odor, as though it had recently been scrubbed with some cheap, strong antiseptic. It accelerated upward with a silent velocity that hollowed his belly and made his knees bend slightly. It opened automatically on a narrower, dingy, old-fashioned corridor. She reached into the elevator as before, and when the door hissed shut and she turned to speak, he said, "I know. There'll be other ways down."

"That isn't what I was going to say."

"I'm sorry. What were you going to say?"

"I can't say it now. You spoiled it."

Again he followed her. These corridors were set at odd angles. The room doors were shiny dark with old coats of varnish. The room numbers were not removed and they were of tarnished brass, fluted and curly and ornate. All the rooms were in the 4000 series, but they were not in any reasonable order, 4100 and something across from or next door to 4800 and something.

She stopped very abruptly; and as he came upon her, he heard what she had heard—the gritty sound of latch and bolt—and then, 20 feet ahead of them, an old couple, dressed for winter, came out of one of the rooms, complaining at each other, fussing, asking if he or she had forgotten this or that, dropping small packages and picking them up.

Just before the old couple turned and noticed them, Mrs. Dorn hooked her arm around his waist and forced him into a slow walk. He put his arm, interlocked, around her, and she reached up with her free hand, placed it against his cheek, chuckled in a furry way, turned her mouth up to the awkward kiss while walking, so that as they passed the couple, he heard tsks and clucks of their disapproval. "Darling, darling," she murmured. "Dave, darling."

Behind them he heard the old man's voice, without

making out the words. There was a harsh resonance to it and then it cracked into a high quaver and then went deep again.

He smiled inside himself, thinking it sounded exactly like Ricky trying to manage his 14-year-old voice as it alternately squeaked and rumbled. The finger tips of the arm that was around her waist touched the top of the pocket on the left side of the gray shift, and with sneaky and daring inspiration, he slid his hand down into the pocket, bending his knees inconspicuously to lower himself just enough, the palm of his hand against round, warm thigh under fabric, and with his finger tips he touched the cylinder of yellow chalk and then the thin edge of metal. With the metal held against the nail of his index finger by the pad of his middle finger, he drew it out of the deep pocket and worked it into the palm of his hand.

She stopped and turned and leaned against the corridor wall and, with her hands resting lightly on his shoulders, looked up at him, still mocking him, saying, "You're just not very bright, Dave, darling."

The old people were gone, around a distant corner of the old hallway. Suddenly, he realized that she had cleverly kept them from seeing his face, so that they would be unable to identify him later. And with a sense of disbelief, he realized she had called him by his name.

"You could have told me how much you knew about this," he said.

"It's better for you to guess, dear. Now look at what you took."

He opened his palm and saw the miniature gold tag. Name, rank, serial number, blood type O, meaning zero, meaning blood type nothing. The shock was enormous. He was suddenly afraid he might cry like a child and shame himself in front of her. "How did you . . . ? How could Leo have . . . ?"

"Leo? Don't be silly. I had it all along. There were always two, you know. Don't you remember that, even? No, keep it, dear. If I have to have it back, you can always give it to me. Without any fuss. Promise?"

"Sure, but if you could just tell me. . . ."

"I can show you, Dave. Come along."

She paused at the next turning and bit her lip and, standing beside her, he saw that the floor itself dipped down in a gentle curve and lifted again at another place in the distance, where it turned again. It was swaying slightly, the whole corridor, like the bridges primitive peoples wove across deep swift rivers. She told him to walk carefully and stay close to the corridor wall. She motioned to him to stop and they were, he saw, on either side of a double door. It was Room 4242. If she knew the rest of it, she would know the right number. It had been so placed that half of it was on each door, so that each was labeled 42. Even though she knew, he did not want her to watch what had to be done, watch the task assigned him; but before he could ask her to go away, to give him the key and go away, go back and wait for him around the corner, out of sight, she put a bright-red key in the lock and the double doors opened inward.

Inward, but outward. They opened onto the nothing of a dizzy height, making a vent for a cold wind that came husking down the hallway behind him and pushed him a long, clumsy stride to stand on the very brink. Far, far, far below, the bug shapes of city cars and trucks moved very slowly, as when seen from an aircraft. He teetered, toes over the edge, and slowly fought back the sickness and the terror, knowing he could not let her see that he suddenly realized how cynically and savagely they had tricked him. He adjusted himself to the slight sway of the corridor and rode it easily, smiling and casual for her benefit, aware of how narrowly she was watching him.

Then came a deep and powerful thud, more vibration than sound. It came welling up from below and it danced the swaying corridor, nearly toppling him out. It came again and again. He learned to ride the new motion. The girl whimpered. He looked far down, almost directly down, and said, "It's nothing. Your friends have come to work. They've got some kind of a derrick thing down there and they're swinging one of those big cannon balls against the foundation."

He stepped back with care and reached and took her hand. Her hand was cold and hesitant. He led her past the open and windy space and back to where, once again, the structure was solid underfoot, trembling almost imperceptibly to each subsonic thud. She pulled her hand free and, after walking slowly, looking at the room numbers, chose one and opened the door, motioning him to come in. The room was in semidarkness, gray light outlining the window. She closed the door and he heard her sigh.

Reaction made him feel weak and sick. He saw the shape of the bed and moved to it and sat on the edge of it. She came to him and pushed at his shoulder and he lay back, grateful that she understood. He swung his legs onto the bed and she went to the foot and unlaced his shoes and took them off.

"We'd better not make very much noise," she whispered.

"Of course."

"Do you understand about the old people?"

"I know that there's something I'm supposed to understand."

"That's enough for now."

She disappeared in the shadows and then he saw her again in silhouette in front of the gray of the window. He heard her sigh and he saw her, with slow and weary motion, tug the shift off over her head, toss it aside, pat her rumpled hair back into order, then bend and slip her shoes off. She stood near the corner of the window, half turned, standing quite still in silhouette, hips in relaxed and weary tilt, and he remembered one of the girls in that Degas print standing off at the side, standing in exactly the same position.

He knew she would turn and come to him but would not understand about what the weakness had done to him. He did not want to confess that kind of weakness to her.

He said, "Even when they do very tricky things, that doesn't mean the rules are changed. We have to follow the rules, just as if everything were happening to someone else, to some people they want to keep, instead of to us. You did it their way, and you know there isn't really any other way down from here. This is all we have left."

"So if I knew all along?" she asked, prompting him.

"If you knew how it was going to be, then you had to know you were a part of it, too."

Not turning, still standing at the gray of the window, she said sadly, softly, "See? You keep understanding more and more of it. Sleep for a little while, darling. Then you'll know the rest of it."

• • •

At a few minutes past six, Dr. Samuel Barringer opened the door of Room 11 in the intensive-care section. In the shadows of the room, he saw the young nurse standing in silhouette by the gray of the window, looking out, standing there with a look of wistful grace.

At the sound of the latch as he closed the door, she spun with a guilty start, greeted him in her gentle and formal morning voice and handed him the clipboard with the patient's chart and the notation she had made since his visit four hours earlier. He held it under the low light for a moment, handed it back to her, then reached through the orifice in the transparent side of the oxygen tent to gently place the pads of his first two fingers against the arterial throb in the slack throat. He stood in a half bow, his eyes closed, listening and measuring through his finger tips. He was a big blond bear of man, simultaneously clumsy and deft, as bears can be.

The nurse stood, awaiting instructions. He told her he would be back in a few minutes and he walked to the far end of the corridor, to the waiting room beyond the nurses' station. Sylvia sat alone there, at the end of the couch by the lamp table, staring out the big window. The hospital tower was higher than the buildings to the west of it, and she could see the wide, slow river in the morning haze. Daylight muted the yellow glow of the lamp beside her.

She turned and saw him and suddenly her dark eyes looked enormous and her face was more pale. "Sam? Is——"

"They didn't call me back. I just came in and checked him, and I have a couple of others to check, and it's standard procedure, Sylvie. No perceptible change."

He walked past her to the big window and shoved his fists into his hip pockets. He stood looking out at the new day.

After a little while, she said, "He's been trying to take it easier since that little coronary. He really has.

But you know how Dave is. He said he was going to weed his practice down to about eight very rich and nervous old ladies with minor ailments. Sam?"

He turned and looked at her, at the lean, mature vitality of her face. "What, honey?"

"What's the prognosis, Sam?"

He shrugged his bear shoulders. "Too early to tell." He looked out the window and saw a freighter being nudged into the channel by the tugs. He wished he were on it and that everybody on board was sworn never to tell Dr. Barringer where they were going or how long they'd be gone.

"Sam, please! That was a big one. Oh, God, I know that was a big one! Remember me, Sam? Eighteen years we three have known one another. I'm a nurse . . . was a nurse. Remember? You don't have to pat me on the head, Sam."

It was easy to remember the Sylvie Dorn of 18 years ago, that chunky, flirtatious, lively girl, now a whip-slender matron, dark hair with the first touches of gray. Thirty-eight? Mother of Ricky, Susan, Timmy—godmother to his own pair of demons. And Dave is—was—is 42.

"Sam?" she said again.

He turned from the window and went lumbering to the couch, thinking of all the times you make this decision and then decide how to wrap words around it to match the person you tell. But this one was close to the past and all the years, close to the heart.

He sat beside her and took her hands and swallowed a rising thickness in his throat, blinked, swallowed again and said in a pebbly voice, "I'm sorry, Sylvie. Dave hasn't got enough heart muscle left to run a toy train. And there's not one damned thing we can do about it or for it."

She pulled her hands free and lunged against him, and he held her in his big arms and patted her as she strained at the first great hard spasmodic sob and got past it and in about two or three minutes pulled herself back to a control and a forlorn stability he knew she would be able to maintain.

She dabbed her eyes and blew her nose and said, "Today sometime?"

"Probably."

"Tell them you've given permission for me to stay in there with him, will you?"

"Of course. I'll be in every once in a while."

"And thank your dear gal for taking over our tribe, Sam. Sam? Do you think he'll know I'm . . . I'm there with him?"

First, he thought, you throw the stone and then you throw the lump of sugar. No point in telling her that death had occurred, that Dave, as Dave, was long gone and that the contemporary miracles of medical science were keeping some waning meat alive, in the laboratory sense of the word.

"From everything we can learn and everything we can guess, Sylvie, I feel certain that he'll be aware of you being there, holding his hand."

• • •

When the first gray light of the morning made the shape of the window visible, he dressed quickly and went out. He guessed that they would not be expecting him to leave that room so soon after arriving.

There were shadows of night still remaining in the empty streets, so that even though he knew his way and walked swiftly, the city seemed strange to him.